BIG

HAM

By

JACOB MCMASTER-BIGUM

BIG HAM

CHAPTER 1

At 1:00 a.m. I am lying shirtless on the floor of my room bench-pressing a pale blue Rubbermaid container full of books when I notice the pile of insects in the globe of the ceiling fan above me. The ceiling fan is going full blast, trying to shake itself loose from the wooden beam it's screwed into, jostling the drifts of ambitious ladybugs that dared to fly over the top and into the surrogate sun I keep burning all night in my room. Ladybugs—red bugs dabbed with black—fight their way inside the light only to obscure it when they die in piles at the bottom of the globe. Lightning bugs—black bugs etched with red—make pinging leaps that briefly lit the inside of the Mason jars I used to catch them in when I was like eight years old. Mom told me then how lightning bugs are incandescent, and, so precociously, right as I was about to scoop one out of the air I said, "Well, they're about to make their in jar descent," and that was the night that Mom and Dad decided that I might be a genius and when the world decided that I would forever remain a virgin.

I'm not worried about being a virgin anymore since I fell in love with Naomi, though. In fact, just thinking about her makes me more compassionate for whatever bugs might still be alive in the bulb, and I slide the Rubbermaid container off my sweaty chest and onto the floor. I carefully step into the half-filled container and reach up to loosen the screws that hold the bulb in place. I swirl the still warm bowl around, panning for any nuggets of still-breathing bugs, but out of the hundreds of ladybug husks there is only one still alive, picking its way over and occasionally sliding down the dunes of its dead brethren, spoiled for choice about whom to die and dry out against. I take the bulb downstairs and dump it off the front porch, and while the bugs sprinkle toward the ground, the last one alive flies clear, looping up and around and over my shoulder until it lands on the face of the halogen bulb blazing in the eaves of the back corner of the porch.

Back up in my room I decide to try some sit-ups, but the damp fat of my back makes an instant vacuum seal with the spaces in between the floorboards, and when I fart upward on my second sit-up, I reach back to touch the foot-long tuft of fuzzy dust, a disgusting ridge of lint interspersed with popcorn kernels left over from the phase at the beginning of the summer where I thought that just eating popcorn would help me lose weight, only I didn't eat diet or plain popcorn, just bags and bags of microwaveable buttered popcorn.

Then I would pour out whatever unpopped kernels were left at the bottom of the bag into an empty soda can and tear the bag into individual strips so that I could lick the coarse salt and butter substitute from the unwrapped armpit bandages of an ancient butter mummy, leaving my jaw as yellow as the bottom half of my Super Nintendo, which I had also stacked inside the pale blue Rubbermaid container. The Super Nintendo and a hardbound copy of Sun Tzu's *Art of War* have been sliding into each other with every unsteady lift like tables on the deck of a wind-tossed ship. Whenever I mention something from *Art of War*, I always say "Sun Tzu's *Art of War*" as if it could be easily confused with Shaquille O'Neal's *Art of War* because, let's face it, I'm kind of a dick.

This popcorn phase came before I got my job as an usher at the movie theater. Though now if I wanted to, I could bring home as much of the stuff as I wanted; I could even take a whole trash bag of day-old popcorn home and cause the girls behind concession to finally have to make it fresh for the matinee crowd. Well, actually, I didn't get the job; my sister got it for me because she had worked there in concession last year and put in a good word for me with Mrs. Clemens, the manager. When Julie came home and told me to go in for an interview, I was initially pretty upset. I had hoped this to be another nothing summer where the only chore I helped out with was unloading the groceries on Sunday afternoon, but Dad had gotten pretty upset with how lazy he perceived me as being. I told him that I would do more chores, that I would finally get around to fixing Mom's printer as promised, and he said, "The first thing that printer spits out will be your résumé, because you're sixteen and you have got to get a goddamned job."

So I did, and I mean, it's easy. Being an usher is like the ultimate starter job. The qualifications are basically to be a monkey with manners. You don't start work before 10:00 a. m. at the earliest, so that means I'm asleep while the rest of the family goes to work, and when I get home Julie's still out and the parents are already in bed, so I don't have to see them for the entire summer. And all you do is clean a couple theaters and sometimes the bathrooms and tear tickets. But in the meantime, you can watch whatever movies are playing, and I even read at the bright red ticket-taker podium for hours straight. Plus up until this week I've gotten to work alongside Naomi. I knew Naomi way before working with her at the theater because she also goes to school with me at Stonewall Academy, but this is the first year when I really seemed to *see* a girl, and that girl is Naomi, and though at this moment only I am in love with her, *we* are about to be in love when she gets back from her trip to Scotland. She took this last week off from work to go there, and during this week I am really going to concentrate on improving my body before she gets back. I have work at ten tomorrow so I had better get to sleep.

I wake up at ten fifteen, and while I remembered to wash my work shirt, it hasn't dried all the way so the cuffs are still damp, and this helps to darken the yellow butter stains there from when concession gets too busy and they call the employees they normally wouldn't trust with food or money up to the front. I can't stand the way they feel on my wrists, and I will have to drive to work with my left arm out the window in the sunshine, my pale forearm trailing unbuttoned and flapping buttered cuffs. I feel my forehead for the pimples I know have grown there overnight. I don't need the mirror, I could pop them in the dark just by feeling the almost painful pressure differentials, the failure Braille on the pockmarked manuscript of my face. My mirror wouldn't do me any good either because it's covered in stickers, most of them from trips to the dentist or the optometrist. Why did my parents spend all this money on my eyes and teeth so that I could see with 20/20 vision a reflection that I will never smile at? I live in a log cabin, but I don't want to talk about it. I grab some Pop-Tarts for the ride into town.

The best way to describe my love for Naomi is through a theory Mr. Welker told us about in physical science. Supposedly, some scientists think that if you split a photon in two, one half of the particle will always instantly mimic the other half's spin, no matter how far apart the two parts of the particle are. Well, that's how it feels, that since Naomi left for Scotland there's been this cache of halvéd love light in my brain and that across the pond the mind behind Naomi's eyes is buzzing with a complimentary set of widowed photons that spin in anticipation for the moment when we're reunited on the first day back at school. Maybe we will hug, maybe we will kiss, maybe we'll be thinking about how advanced scientific principles are often naively and inappropriately applied to emotional or spiritual situations, and we'll look at each other across a crowded courtyard and *know*.

Naomi's pretty much in charge of concession. Mrs. Clemens likes her so much that she lets Naomi wear non-regulation shirts at work, and Naomi often wears a purple, long-sleeve shirt that kind of shimmers. They sell these shirts like hers in the outlet store next door, and after work today I think I'll go by and make a few passes past the rack so I can run my hand over the sleeves. Not because I'm perverted, it's just that I need to prepare my brain for the process of touching Naomi. If I can gradually eliminate extraneous sensations—the fabric of her shirt, the glint on the bangs of her short brown hair, the slight baby powder smell to her—then I won't be overwhelmed by the time I get to her skin and will avoid doing something creepy like giggling or passing out.

It's not like Naomi's inaccessible at school. She often spends most of her time sitting with our group. It just took a summer of working with her to realize how strongly I feel for her. Besides, I just couldn't get a chance to talk with her before. Though she's smart enough to sit with us, she's pretty enough to fit in anywhere. In fact, last year she was dating the most awesome guy at our school, James Reynolds, until he had a kind of heart attack and died during a basketball game, right in the middle of the gym floor, and you could hear his head crack against the school seal. So, last year dating her was totally not an option. Naomi's recovered since then. Before she left I caught her making out with Lawrence in the theater's lost and found. I never actually saw them kiss though. There are a million different reasons why he might have had both his thumbs hooked into her belt loops.

When I finally get to the theater and back to the break room, Mrs. Clemens is already standing there. Instead of talking to her, I go over to the sign-in sheet, hoping that by bending over and signing my name I'll have adopted the most eager to work and nonconfrontational posture possible in this situation.

"You're late," she says, not saying my name because she doesn't know it. When she yells at my coworkers, she always uses their names. The nametag she gave me when I started just says "Trainee." It is shaped like one of those clapper boards that say "Take __" that are clapped before a director yells "Action."

"At least your shirt's clean today," continues Mrs. Clemens as I continue to slowly write a name she'll never learn. "But now your undershirt's dirty. I can't have you walking around my theater with a dirty undershirt."

"It's not dirty. It's just got writing on it," I say. On my under-shirt are the names of last year's class officers when I was elected vice president, running unopposed. Mrs. Clemens would let Nate or Lawrence, the other ushers, get away with this, but she writes numerous procedural notes and tapes them to the hot dog turner or the ICEE machine, and they're always horribly misspelled or have terrible grammar, and one day she caught me correcting them with a Sharpie marker. So, surprise, she hates me because she thinks I think that I'm smarter than she is. And…I…am…

"I don't care writing…dirty…doesn't matter," she says. "Go on to the outlet store next door. They've got shirts that will fit Miranda there. I'm sure they have ones that will fit a boy like you."

For a moment I stand there quietly, and there's no sound but her breathing and the hissing coming from the bloated silver ticks of soda syrup being carbonated and pumped up to the front, and then I say, "OK, I will. I'm sorry Mrs. Clemens," and walk out of the room and back behind concession and further back to the ticket-taker podium where I will stay all day because Mrs. Clemens will forget me and be yelling at the concession girls and getting calls yelling at her from the branch manager.

Lawrence is sitting next to the ticket-taker podium on the stacks of children's booster seats, the hollow, stackable, pri-mary colored ones with little Velcro strips on the bottom to keep the kids from sliding off the seats. People only ask for them once or twice a day, so there's always a sitable stack. Lawrence is always sitting, either in the theaters or on the booster seats or on the popcorn bags piled up in the break room. If I ever come in at night when Lawrence has been working that afternoon, there are two distinct indentions in the top bag where his ass has been. Every single one of the girls in concession is in love with him. They joke how he could pop the bag that he's sitting on simply by the heat generated from his buttocks. He's black and about a foot taller than I am and strong as all get out. He can carry two forty pound bags over each shoulder from the stock room. He can't lift them all up by himself though; he has to get Nate, another usher, to lift the last two bags up and onto his shoulders.

Then he swaggers back to the break room and has the girls behind concession take it down for him like those seed sacks are four freshly clubbed gazelles, their mouths open and lolling over his shoulder, an unnaturally large bounty for their upsizing tribe. By the way, I didn't use those singularly African analogies because he's black or because I consider him primitive. I just want to say that right up front.

Lawrence is quiet, but I think that's because he has a slight lisp and he's embarrassed and that if he didn't have that lisp he'd be just as loud and as callous as Nate.

"You mithed the retards," says Lawrence as I take one time and one time only to type out how he sounds. Sometimes a whole group of mentally disabled people comes to watch the summer matinees, and I'm the only usher who can keep his composure while tearing their tickets. On certain days Lawrence might be able to keep himself from laughing, but Nate absolutely cannot. He has to stay in the utility closet beside the podium and bite his hand to keep from giggling while playing games on his cell phone. When the retards leave, Nate stumbles out with the empty lost and found box over his head and shouts "I'm lost! I'm lost!" in his best mooning retard. He does this now.

"I'm lost! I'm lost!" says Nate as he comes out of the utility closet, waving his arms around. Honestly I can't help but laugh a little, even though last week Nate found the one story in my sci-fi anthology that I had hidden in the lost and found that mentioned alien sex and read aloud from it to all the girls behind concession.

"Big Ham, the kids just left from theater two, so how about you clean it," says Lawrence being the boss of me.

"Lawrence, you are not the boss of me," I say.

"Just do it, Big Ham," says Lawrence. "Nate can help. There were like two busloads from that summer camp."

"No thanks, I'll do it myself," I say, getting a mini-broom and dustpan from the utility closet. In theater two there's this one seat that some kid pooped in last week that still has a trash bag duct-taped to it, and whenever I clean that theater with Nate or Lawrence, they always try to push me into it. Gosh, what would Naomi see in someone like Lawrence to allow him to make out with her in the utility closet until her back brushed against the bank of light switches and made an entire interrupted audience mimic the sound my heart made when I found them?

But I don't care how far Lawrence got with her. I can't help the way I feel about Naomi. Even if she got back from Scotland and I found out that Lawrence had made her pregnant, I would still care for her, I would stick with her, I would raise my bully's babies to get close to Naomi because she's the only girl I've ever seen who understands.

She's also the only one who notices things at the theater, like the time when an errant unpopped kernel had rolled into one of the floor drains behind the concession stand and a delicate, white-green stalk began to poke its way out amid the shuffling black-shoed threshers of half a dozen college dropouts and remedial readers. When she kneeled down to yank it out, I stopped sweeping for a minute and watched her face in profile in the only light I like in that theater—the gold glowing from the popcorn machine beside her. She's so pretty and she wears a necklace of black lace around where he Adam's apple would be if she were a female impersonator, and I just want to run my index finger under it so much that I almost miss seeing the child seat velcroed to the wall of theater two.

Ugh, I hate those kids. They make the worst messes possible in both the theaters and the bathrooms, and they almost bowl me over when they run down the main aisle of the theater. Every thirty minutes of a showing an usher has to go into a theater and check that it the picture looks fine and that nobody's making sweeps over the stars' faces with a laser, and those summer camp kids always look over to me and make it clear that they do not like me. My only saving grace is that in their minds I am white before I am fat, and if I leave right after they call me white boy, I can avoid their more specific insults.

On the floor below the booster seat that's stuck to the wall is yet *another* booster seat that, true to its nature, provided the boost the kid needed to slap that hollow plastic box against the wall. I walk up and rip the other booster seat off the wall only to find out that this kid, in a fit of Wile E. Coyote genius, has filled it with trash, including the cold red remnants of his cherry ICEE that spills across my back like frozen blood. Not just ICEE either, but whatever spare bits of trash and food that he could find on the floor of the theater, including an almost fist-sized ball of mashed-together Skittles with their colored shells sucked off, a gritty, granulated chewed tumor that lay malignant in that kid's mouth until he spit it into the upturned booster seat so that it would fall down into my collar and against my neck, retaining the same sickening consistency of my own fat-curdled kneecaps. God! God, if I could only catch him!

I must have shouted in surprise because Lawrence walks in and starts laughing at me.

"Damn, man, you look..."

"What, Lawrence? What do I look? Sthhhtupid? Sthhhilly?" I ask, imitating his lisp.

At this Lawrence walks up real close to me, real close, so that he almost touches my belly, and he stretches forward a little, and his head hovers over mine as if he's about to dart down and peck me with his chin. He stares straight ahead.

"Maybe you should take the trash outside," says Lawrence and just stands there for a few seconds until I turn around and roll the theater's first can out from the recessed space in the wall and through the middle of the theater and around to the other entrance and grab the second can and wheel them both down the main hallway and outside toward the sunlight and Dumpsters.

I immediately regret my sibilant disobedience because I feel bad for making fun of Lawrence and because he doesn't usually make fun of me and I could really use his help taking the heavy bags out of the cans. I can't yank them straight up like he can. I can only tip the cans onto their sides and drag the bags out. Outside of the toothachingly cool theater, I immediately begin to perspire, and the cold soda sloshing in the bottom of the trash bags means that they too are soon coated in a layer of sympathetic sweat. I stand there looking out over the heat-shimmered K-Mart parking lot across the street, two trash bags acting as discarded armless torsos lying in the weed tufts and brown beer bottle shards poking up between the cracked asphalt at my feet. While getting up the energy to lift the bags into the Dumpster, I look like I'm winding down an exhausting day in the showroom of the torso store, other models strewn about my feet, and that the lumpy one I'm wearing is the one I finally settled on. Or rather, it had settled onto me.

With a weak, whiny second cousin to a grunt, I hoist the first bag up above my knees, over my stomach, and up to my chest, gonging it barely over the bottom lip of the open side door of the Dumpster.

The next bag is much heavier, gurgling with ice, soaked popcorn, and the soggy cardboard of kiddie trays, candy boxes, and cups. I've got half of it hunched into the Dumpster and I'm pushing up on its sagging ass, fearing that the bag will split open at the bottom and spill its innards all over an already irrevocably ruined shirt, and when the bag finally chunks to the bottom of the Dumpster, I think for a brief second that I should heave myself in after it, like the Dumpster is a boxcar that will carry me and my chubby younger brothers away from the theater and on to freedom and the slimming, muscle-hardening work of the Midwest.

Lawrence opens the door behind me and looks out, his pupils dilating closed at the flood of sunlight while his nostrils dilate open at the steel fruit smell of the Dumpsters.

"Lawrence, I'm sorry for making fun of you. I was just mad after getting that ICEE on me," I say.

"You are always apologizing, man. It's fine," says Lawrence. "You need to come up front because your little friend's hitting on all the girls and isn't buying anything. He doesn't even have a ticket."

"OK, I'm coming up to get him."

CHAPTER 2

Travis McCullen admitted we were best friends a little over two years ago, when both our parents decided to send us to Stonewall. We hung out a lot in the same group when we first started high school, but Travis still remained best friends with a guy from his old middle school because he was absolutely infatuated with the guy's stepsister. Travis said she was the first girl who wouldn't let him kiss her, but she was also the first girl he'd ever tried to kiss. After a while there was a whole new crop of girls to come on to, and both the old best friend and the stepsister were forgotten. Travis has come on to almost every girl at Stonewall except for Naomi because he said that he "respected James Reynolds's sovereignty." Now with James gone, I can only hope that Travis will leave Naomi alone just because he doesn't want to hear me plead.

While walking up to the front of the theater, I see Travis leaning over the concession counter, the lower three bumps of his spine poking out from the bottom of his black T-shirt, his fingers tapping on the glass. Travis's black hair hangs down to his shoulders because he doesn't cut it during the summer, partly because he loves making a huge deal about when "Christian fascists" that he says run Stonewall make him cut it on the first week of school, and partly because right after he gets his head shaved girls come up and rub it.

"Big Ham, it's about time," says Travis.

"Travis, I hate it when you use my school nickname at my work," I said. "Now everybody here calls me Big Ham."

"Big Ham, if you meet someone who learns what your last name is, then looks at you, and they don't instantly come up with that nickname, then they're not worth knowing. Besides, it is going to happen anywhere. It's convergent nickname evolution," Travis says.

"Oh, wow, evolution," I say. "You know they're going to beat that out of you at Stonewall—right after they make you shave your head."

"Yeah, I know," says Travis. "I'm working on my mustache too to see just how many things they make me change on the first day back. Where were you anyway? I asked that black dude to go get you like fifteen minutes ago."

"Lawrence and I aren't getting along today," I say, "and I was outside dumping the trash."

"Did you do that to yourself or did Lawrence throw you into the Dumpster?" Travis asks.

"No, it happened in the theater," I say. "Look, Travis, why are you even here? I can't get you in for free again because

Mrs. Clemens already yelled at me today and I still have work for like three more hours."

"Dude, I don't need you to get me into the theater. I'll just scamper around you and then what are you going to do? Are you going to throw me out? Besides, I can't go anywhere. My parents dropped me off to see a movie and hang out with you, and after that I do need you to drive me to Heather's birthday party," Travis says.

"If your parents dropped you off here they could have dropped you off at that party," I say.

"Big Hammmmm," he says, stretching the "m", "I'm not going to get out of my parents' car at this party. Not like showing up with you is any better. But then you get to come! You get to party before school starts and grab some free pizza and then maybe find a chubby girl with which to get your fuck on," Travis says. It's then that I notice the white nylon umbilical peeking out of the top of his jeans.

"Travis is this a pool party? Because you know how much I love pool parties," I say. Travis is obsessed with evolution but wants to put me an environment where I'm guaranteed to fail?

"There will be a pool at this party, yes," says Travis. "But it's not like you have to swim. Not like you have to put on your widdle water wings and paddle awound," he says, pulling the tops of both sleeves away from my chicken-fried triceps and shaking me back and forth with all his skinny-kid strength until I laugh and push him away.

"Travis, I don't think I've been to any other party all summer, so it's not like I have to squeeze one more great bash in before all my freedom is taken away or anything. All parties blow, you know that," I say.

"Bigham, just take me there. You don't have to stay. Just come in and say hi to Heather because she's in charge of the yearbook, and you know you like to write those little captions. I'll find someone else to take me home," says Travis. He looks past me to the sign that shows the theater numbers and times like a stock ticker. "Until you get off, though, I'll be in theater eight, maybe eleven if you're not off by the time that show ends."

Travis takes a quick look around for Mrs. Clemens, who he knows from when he applied earlier this summer but wasn't hired because he made even less of an effort to be interested during his interview than I did. Travis sees that the coast is clear and breaks into a little jog that says "I have never taken part in organized sports of any kind" and goes down the main corridor, sandals slapping the bottom of his feet, and long hair bobbing up behind him.

Three hours later in an empty theater eight Travis helps me pick up the bigger cups and popcorn bags from off of the floor, and he finds one bag that's half full and tightly folds down the top so he can eat out of it later. It's my last theater to clean, and I sign out without saying good-bye to anybody, except Miranda, the woman who will probably work in the box office until she dies. Miranda is the only person here who's talked to me for any amount of time. She is fantastically fat, and she always talks about being tired or her feet hurting with a short laugh and a weak punch to my shoulder, saying, "People like us understand each other, right?" I had hoped that when she says "people like us" she thinks that I too have tried to escape from a brutal post-menopausal depression by spending several paychecks getting certified in reflexology, but she just means that I belong in the same fat strata of people that make our state dark red in the obesity surveys in *USA Today*.

"Bye, Miranda," I say and wave to her in the booth as Travis and I walk across the parking lot to my truck.

"Oh, bye, Jacob," Miranda says into the microphone.

"I wasn't even invited to this party anyway," I tell Travis on the way there.

"Sure you were," says Travis, eating popcorn. "She posted on her away message about her party. She said everyone who was going to be in the junior class could come. The only reason I got an invitation was because she knew me from when I went to her church," he says, pulling out a piece of paper that's been folded four times into a card, a big pink "16" its front.

"You know that away message still didn't mean guys like me."

"Well, she's still not going to throw you out. I took you on that Carowinds thing with my church and she was there, and she'll also know you from school." Travis puts his pack of cigarettes on my dashboard to avoid crushing it in his back pocket. His brother brings him a pack once and a while when he comes down from summer school. Travis has to pace himself so that he can save cigarettes for public appearances, smoking one every other day in the woods behind his house to keep his lungs from getting rusty. He's only got half a pack left for tonight. I'm sure I'll see him make exaggerated movements to hide them from Heather's parents, loaning out one or two with whispered speeches of how *you totally cannot get caught with this.*

"So everybody in our class is going to be there?"

"Almost everybody. Plus all Heather's friends from when she went to Birchwood Christian are going to be there. Plus all three of Heather's former boyfriends, so that means Connor. But I know how much you hate him. He'll arrive way late though, and you can be gone by then."

Connor had also been on that trip to Carowinds in the church van at the beginning of the summer. It had been hot going from ride to ride at the park, and Connor had always made sure to wipe his face with the front hem of his shirt, making sure to lean back, bunch up his shoulders, and suck in so that the girls in the group could see the muscles in his stomach. He would encircle his arms around Heather and steady her laser gun in the arcade, bolstering her against recoil that didn't exist with his burgeoning boner. And when he gave Heather the souvenir picture of himself as a Confederate soldier, a soldier with stray spikes of gelled hair peeking out from under his cap, a soldier whose soulful, sepia-stained stare spoke of boy bands existing before lightbulbs and Heather reacted to the picture as if he really was going off to fight for the South the next day. They could not keep their hands off each other for the entire ride home. Geez, if your face is sweating, just wipe it with your sleeve or even your collar. Don't lift up the entire tail.

I don't hate Connor. In fact, sometimes he's kind of cool. I heard he almost went to jail this summer because he had an emergency radio scanner in his car, and whenever he heard about a fire he would drive to the scene and steal a single piece of firefighter equipment—just a boot or a gas mask at a time, and he had most of the whole ensemble and was already up to the ax when he was finally caught. His dad probably did some good ol' boy string pulling and kept Connor out of jail. Connor's dad owns both a Mazda dealership and a mobile home dealership that stand across from each other on the sides of the highway into town, so Connor's rich and is guaranteed the best of almost-homes and almost-sports cars for the rest of his life and doesn't even have to finish high school if he doesn't want to.

Connor's never outright bullied me, but every year on Valentine's Day the cheerleaders do a fundraiser where you can send candy or a carnation to someone else in the school for a dollar, and of course, I never got one until last year when a palm-sized chocolate heart was left on my desk by a girl who had to ask the class who I was, and the note that came with it said, "From the people who make candy, thanks for all your support." And I know, I know it was Connor because he laughed so hard when I got up to throw it in the trash. Also, when I was waiting in line to get a hot dog at homecoming, Connor nudged ahead of me in line, but James Reynolds, who was working the grill because of a sprained ankle, made a point of looking past him and asking me what I wanted. But this has been the extent of Connor's dickitude toward me and really, I deserve it. By being mean to me about food, he's only telling me what people like Naomi are too nice to say: that I need to get in shape because in a little over a year I'm going to turn eighteen and I don't want to be allowed into manhood based solely on a genital technicality. I want to be, you know, strong and everything. I'm just grateful for the fact that now I'm motivated by something purer than a peal of Connor's laughter.

Heather's house is in one of the suburbs on the outskirts of town near Stonewall. She's in the middle house at the end of a circle. There are already a couple cars here even though we're a little early, and it's still bright out at six o'clock.

"OK," Travis says. "Just come in for a second and tell Heather happy birthday and ask her about the yearbook."

I park on the side of the circle, and Travis grabs his pack of cigarettes, gets out before me, and heads over to the front door of Heather's house. Standing and small-barking at him from behind the screen door is a cocker spaniel, the fur graying around its eye sockets, its wagging tail causing the fat on its back to shift back and forth in a single sheet. Well, it's not a screen door, we have a screen door. This is just a second door with plastic windows, a nictitating membrane that protects the house from irritants like Travis and me.

Anyways, I'm grateful to see it because little dogs always give me something to do at parties rather than talk to people. A forty-five-year-old Heather stands in the hallway with her left hand on her hip, the other arm pointing out to her side, pointer finger outward while her other fingers curve around a half-filled glass of white wine.

"Party's in the back, guys," she yells over the barking. Dust motes buzz around the sides of her white capri pants as if the nutrients they need to survive are being pumped through her panty lines. As she shouts the sentence at us, her second chin, pearl necklace, and the dog's back reach a weird, wobbling synchronicity. Travis gives a little wave and smiles while hiding the cigarettes behind his back and walks over to the fence, reaches over and unlatches its gate, and I follow him into the party.

Heather and her two friends are the only ones there. Heather and her plain friend are hanging Chinese lanterns from the rain gutter while Heather's fat friend is in a chair under the umbrella of the patio table swatting mosquitoes away from her legs with a rolled up *Cosmopolitan*.

"Hey, Heather," I say while Heather strings another lantern under the gutter.

Heather looks down at me from the step stool and waves, "Oh, hey, Jacob, I'm glad you could come," she says. Heather has like this really professional voice and always sounds like she has her shit together and is happy to talk to whoever she's talking to at the time, even me.

"Can you get that other box of lanterns for me?" asks Heather, pointing to a cardboard box in the corner of the patio labeled "Chin Lanterns," and as I walk to get the box, I think that I could tell Heather that I already have a lantern jaw as a way to show how witty I am and maybe be allowed to write more yearbook captions this year.

"So, yeah, Heather, Happy Birthday," I say, handing up the first lantern out of the box and holding the next one on the string in my hands. "Are you excited about editing the yearbook again? Because I really like writing the captions, and I'd like to help out again." I guess this is like networking or something.

"Actually, Jacob, I got some comments on the captions you wrote last year," Heather says, the sun now right above her head so that as I squint up at her I can't make out her exact expression.

"Oh really?" I ask, excited about any recognition.

"Yeah, especially from Mrs. Bailey. She thinks that maybe your jokes were a little too negative or dark, " Heather says, and the sun's corona combines with her blond hair, human form, and undifferentiated facial features to make this the closest I've come to a rebuke from heaven's emissary. "She says that you should go easy on the teasing and the sarcasm, but if you want to lighten it up, sure, you can write some captions," Heather says.

"Um, sure, OK." I say. "No, I can definitely lighten it up," I say, desperate not to lose my only extracurricular activity.

"There's going to be a big tribute page for James since this would have been his senior year," Heather says. "You could definitely submit a couple paragraphs for that."

"I don't know if I could," I say. "I mean, writing about James, I definitely don't want to say anything wrong. Maybe if I like interviewed some seniors who knew him."

"Sure, Jacob, that's a good idea," Heather says, climbing down from the step stool. I hear the fence gate clatter close, and soon there are like twelve more people coming in, and I can hear even more voices outside in the front yard. Travis is uncharacteristically still talking to the fat girl sitting by the patio table who is pulling her swimming skirt closed over her unsunned thighs and holding the *Cosmopolitan* open over the top of her one-piece while the cocker spaniel yaps at her purple painted toenails. Travis is laughing at her jokes and flipping through a huge CD organizer when I tap him on the shoulder and tell him that I'm about to leave.

"OK, OK, Bigham if you're sure you don't want to stay and hang out," says Travis. "Don't worry about me. I can always get a ride home from somebody else."

"I'm sure and OK," I say, and wave to Heather and go to the front yard to find Connor's red Miata parked right beside my truck. My truck is in the first layer of cars parked inside the circumference of the circle, while Connor's car is parked in the second inner layer, and another layer of cars is beginning to form behind that one.

Connor is leaning up against my truck and talking to someone I don't recognize. Connor is wearing, from just the top of his head to his neck, a University of South Carolina hat that says "GO COCKS" on it, a huge gold fishhook bent over the brim of that hat with the hook on the top, red-framed Oakley sunglasses, a tiny diamond earring, a silver stud earring, a black mustache that pours down into his goatee with a cigarette dangling from the lips between them, and a hemp necklace draped over yet another necklace that has a gold cross on it. Connor is flipping open a gold Zippo lighter just as I walk up, a belated Olympic torch making its way to the douchebag decathlon already taking place on his face.

"Dude, thank God you're here," says Connor as I walk up.

"Why, what's wrong?" I ask.

"Aren't you the valet?" asks Connor, pointing at my usher ensemble with his cigarette. The guy beside him laughs.

"No, I just got off work at the theater," I say. "Hey, Connor, do you mind moving your car because I'm not staying."

"I'm blocked in too Big Ham," says Connor, referring to the third circle and the two layers of cars packing the sides of the street like the mercury about to burst from an asphalt thermometer. "Just go back inside and hang out—that's what a party's for. And where did you get that huge stain on your shirt?"

"It's, um, the blood of the last guy who asked me if I was the valet," I say and Connor waves his hands like he's so scared and says "Oooohhh" and his friend laughs harder at my comeback than when Connor first joked about me.

"Connor, who is the guy parked behind you because I have better things to do than impress your friends," I say.

"Big Ham, A: No you don't and B: Good luck getting out of here because even if you find the guy parked behind me, I won't move just because you're acting so tough." And with that Connor brushes past me and through the gate. Only then do I notice a Coke bottle half filled with brown dip spit that *someone* has thrown into the bed of my trapped truck. I am forced to trail behind Connor back into the party, the amorphous, bloodstained ghost of his cologne.

CHAPTER 3

"Connor, you're late!" shouts Heather as she runs up to hug him. She then yanks the cigarette out of his mouth and makes a big deal of stomping it out on the patio, but all the while she is giving Connor a look that says she's lost a purity ring inside herself just thinking about him.

"Connor, you know you can't smoke! My parents might see!" Heather says, using her second exclamation point of the party.

"Hey, Heather, chill out," says Connor. "I just had to pick my little brother up from gifted kid camp. Chill out and Happy Sixteenth Birthday. Now all the things I do to you will be legal," says Connor with more wit than I'd ever given him credit for.

"You know we don't do anything," says Heather and punches him a shoulder unshielded by his sleeveless *No Fear* T-shirt. She keeps her fist there way longer than necessary, her knuckles lingering on the muscle. Connor's arms are tanned and huge. He folds them over his chest while he's talking to Heather and the front of his hands cup under his biceps to push them out even more. There are hints of flint in his elbows that Heather reaches out to touch, gasping in mock pain and sucking on an index finger cut by the parts of Connor that are oh-so-hard and oh-so-sharp.

I sit down at the chair opposite the overweight girl, a little boom box shaking the table between us. Even if we did talk, I'm sure the only thing that we have in common is that over the last few years our parents have watched our bodies blossom into ample womanhood, and while I know that Travis will give me a hard time later about not making overtures to the only girl here in my league, I decide not to waste her time. There's a reason why unattractive people are not attracted to each other.

Instead I sit there like I was paid to watch a pool party movie marathon. There are about thirty kids here, most of them from Stonewall. I have never seen them stand so straight in my life; your spine shifts shape when you're shirtless. I watch Heather climb onto Connor's shoulders in the pool and chicken fight with her plain friend and a guy who's one year into college and really shouldn't be here. I am afraid that Heather's thigh will catch on the fishhook attached to the hat Connor still insists on wearing, but then I overhear some dumb girl ask what "carbs" is short for and almost snap my nametag in half in contempt.

Heather's dad comes out of the house with a stack of pizza boxes, and Travis brings me a slice because he's correctly guessed that I will not give up this seat under any circumstances.

"Dude, are you having any fun at all?" asks Travis.

"Not really, but what did I expect?" I say.

"Dude, watch this," says Travis and walks over to where Connor is standing behind the birthday girl, squeezing her left shoulder with a grade school massage while drinking from a can of Mountain Dew that he sometimes brushes against Heather's back to make her squeal. Now, either Heather hung wind chimes alongside the Chinese lanterns or the sound I hear is Travis's newly bronzed balls banging against each other because Travis walks up to the right side of Heather and begins to massage that shoulder.

"Oh my gosh, Connor, you could learn a thing or two from Travis. That feels great," says Heather. And before Connor can react, Travis's hand almost brushes his aside and usurps the span of soft and sacred girl-shoulder space, leaving a flabbergasted Connor to stare in disbelief as Travis whispers a dirty joke into Heather's ear. It is the highlight of my night.

At midnight Heather's mom bonks her palm against the sliding glass door, and Heather starts saying good-bye. Nobody brought any real gifts—only parents can afford the toys at our age—but a lot of people just stacked envelopes on the end of the card table beside the boxes that hold the greasy cheese ridge stars of eaten pizzas. Everyone is out in front starting up their cars, except for the people who fell in love tonight and are stealing citronella kisses in the four corners of Heather's dying birthday world. Travis is among them; he's latched on to Heather's plain friend and is kissing her beside the gate while I wait against my truck. Connor finally comes to start his car and let me out but not before he says a few choice words.

"I know you two super geniuses are going to joke about how Travis stole that massage from me," says Connor.

"Sure, Connor, you are all we talk about," I say.

"I'm just saying I know how you nerds are, and you get all hung up about what you see is beating guys like me. But after I drive away from here, Heather's going to call me on her cell phone, and in a couple hours I will drive back and bang the hell out of her on her birthday," says Connor, with the grinning certainty of a pack of jackals shooed away from a stillborn giraffe.

"Wow, dude, that's going on page one of the *Connor Chronicle* that Travis and I will stay up all night writing," I say, realizing that this is the second time I've smarted off to a huge dude today, only Connor's not as close to me as Lawrence was. Connor's tone is very matter-of-fact because he and I both know he's right. Connor gets in his car and pulls away just as Travis walks up.

"Guess you're the one taking me home tonight, Bigham."

"I guess so, Travis."

"Good night, Travis, guys," Heather waves as we both leave. "Drive carefully."

"That was pretty awesome when you straight up stole Heather's shoulders from Connor," I say to Travis on the way to his house.

"Yeah, well, I was just glad to be double bagged by my swimsuit or else she would have felt my boner in her back," says Travis, throwing away his cigarette before we pull up to the ID checking station at the gate to the Air Force base. Travis has to unbuckle his seatbelt and lean over me to give the guard his ID, and I can smell smoke and the perfume of every girl he's flirted with in his hair. It's the closest I've been to another human being my age for the entire summer, and I almost get hard, but then we're waved through and the acceleration pushes the blood back into my body.

I don't know how to get around in the dark on the Air Force base, and all the houses look the same, but eventually Travis tells me to stop in front of one of them.

"I guess I'll see you next week when we get back to school, Bigham," says Travis.

"Later," I say.

On the highway home, I pass all the Air Force themed businesses that spring up between a military base and the outskirts of a town that's trying its best to appease it. There's like two barber shops called Hair Force, only the one that opened up a week earlier than the other has "The Original" painted above its name, and the F-16 Tailors, where in past years Mom took my pants to get them hemmed after the supreme irony of shopping at the men's section at JCPenney. When I first started blowing up, Mom had to ask the sales-clerk if there was a husky section, but there wasn't; husky implies some kind of strength, that my girth was more of a side effect of my vitality. They should have had an obese section, the "o" hitting the "b" like a pad of butter on a frying pan and sizzling out of the salesclerk's mouth as he pointed toward it. Plus, whenever Mom would send me in to get my pants, I had to wait in line behind fighter pilots and people who had to look fit and crisp for a living, while I waited for my hacked-off little man's pants.

I turn off the highway and down the last paved road to my house, then onto the dirt road that my driveway feeds into. They just put gravel on the dirt road this morning, and I am unaccustomed to the rumble that my truck makes as I pull into my driveway. My driveway is about a tenth of a mile long and framed on both sides with pine trees planted a year after I was born, and their roots stretch across the driveway and jostle my truck as I drive over them. I am framed by a hundred younger brothers all grown taller than me and tak-ing their time to trip me up as I stumble home. Right before I get to the clearing where my house is, a doe looks up from where she's been eating the grass in between the tire tracks and stares at me, and it's the most intense attention I could hope to receive from a female tonight, and even that's because I was barreling down on her in my truck.

The front porch lights are blazing and cast the rest of the house and yard in deep black shadow. I don't like describing my house, just like I don't like describing my body. When you grow up inside something you hate, you only remember its blemishes. But, I mean, it's two stories of caulked together logs of rain grayed wood. That's about it. Behind the house are all the ruins of things Dad built for Julie and me to exercise on. There's a large circle of sand in a patch of knee-high grass, an anti-oasis where the above ground pool used to be before it was halved by a Hurricane Hugo-blown tree. There's a basketball goal where rotted black remnants of net hang from the rim like teeth rotted by all the sweet shots I never took.

Inside all the downstairs lights are still on, but the TV's off, a single handprint visible in the dust of the screen, as eternal as a boot print in the moon. We only have the lights on and the TV off if company's coming, and now it seems that I am company in my own home.

Dad is still awake and sitting facing me at the end of the kitchen table, which we haven't eaten at as a family since last Thanksgiving, and that's why there's still a locally woven cornucopia made of muscadine vines filled with bright plastic fruit that spill over a stack of rubber banded bills. I know that I am going to be yelled at for not calling, so I go and sit down in the chair across the table from him, my back to the hutch that's filled with my academic plaques from year-end award ceremonies, as a kind of subliminal character witness to the high quality mind he's about to berate.

"Jacob, you know you're in trouble, but do you know why you're in trouble?" asks Dad as he leans back in his chair and folds his arms so that the hairs on his forearms Velcro together over his chest. His right forearm is darker than his left from when he hangs it out the window to deliver mail. This is just one of the many details of my Dad that I have acquired by not looking him in the eye.

"Dad, Travis came by the theater and dragged me to this pool party," I say.

"Jacob, you even have a phone in your truck," Dad says. It's one of those gray brick phones that like have the charger permanently attached.

"Why do we pay for that phone if you're not going to use it? You were gone six hours without calling. Mom and I were just about ready to go out and drive to find you until she thought and called Travis's dad. You're lucky he told his dad where he was."

"I was just going to drop Travis off, but I got blocked in by all the cars and couldn't leave. I just stayed out until eleven; you guys said I could stay out even later than that," I say.

"*If* you called, Jacob. If you called. But when your mom and I don't know *where you are*, we get worried." He points at me or taps on the table at every italics, and I can see myself wincing at each emphasis. He's using the Dad voice and the Dad intonation that makes my eyelids hurt like when he's waking me up to go to school.

"I'm sorry, OK? It was a strange house, and I didn't mean to stay out that late, but next time I'll call."

"Next time, next time, next time. Jacob, you know the rules. A lot of other kids don't have half the freedom you do."

"It's because I don't do anything. You guys never have to worry about me, and you didn't have to worry about me tonight. I don't drink. You'd barely even know I was at that party."

"Jacob—"

"And you don't have to say my name every time you start to say something. I mean, there's nobody else down here. Like I know it's me you're yelling at." But he must feel obligated to say my name over and over because I'm not looking at him. Instead I'm looking at the blue measurement marks the carpenters left on the ceiling beams, like doctors circling cellulite on a surgery makeover show, at a cross-stitch depicting a crib and the day I was born and how much I weighed at birth, even at a picture of Dad when he was young and fresh out of the air force and standing proudly in front of a pile of logs that would eventually become this house—looking anywhere but directly at Dad.

"Jacob, look at me when I'm talking to you," says Dad. "All right, fine. First off, when you start school, your sister can drive you both. You don't need to go in separate cars to the same school, and she's got that senior space this year," says Dad.

"Jesus Christ."

"Well, he ain't here and if he was, he'd be telling you the same thing. Second, after work tomorrow you're going to wash all the cars out there," he says, and this is major because he's talking about his car, Mom's car, Julie's new Mercury Cougar, which I'm not sure she'll even let me wash, my car, and then maybe even his old truck.

"Not the junk truck too, right?" I ask.

"Oh yeah, that truck. And the dog. Use the buckets and sponges under the sink."

"Which sponge do I use on the dog?"

"The one that's got all the dog hair on it."

"Whatever."

"Yeah, whatever, whatever. You have to learn, and I've taught you, that we trust you to stay out because you usually call and tell us where you're going to be. So make sure *alllll* of the cars are clean tomorrow." During the long drawn out "*alllll*" he had stabbed out his fingers in random directions like he was pointing at the cars and trucks in the driveway, but really he just needed to point at something.

"You work until five, right?" Dad asks. I just wish I could have taken a shower after those hours on the patio chair and maybe pulled on a sweatshirt so that I could have had something more substantial between my heart and his voice.

"Yeah, I get off at five," I say.

"I'm serious about this punishment," he says.

"OK, OK, I will clean them. Just can I please go to sleep?" I say.

"You need to go to sleep? I need to go to sleep," says Dad and pushes his chair back and goes upstairs.

CHAPTER 4

Before I go upstairs, I check the fridge for something to eat because, besides the piece of cheese pizza Travis snagged for me at the pool party, I haven't had anything to eat all day. Inside there's a Styrofoam take-home container from Red Lobster with Julie's name written on the top along with the time (8:55) when it was put into the refrigerator. The rules used to be that you had to wait a day for somebody to eat their own leftovers before the food could be declared open season and accessible by anybody in the house, but I had consistently justified waiting a "day" as waiting until the next morning or early afternoon to help myself. Then I could spend all Friday night and Saturday morning playing video games, eat whatever Julie or Mom hadn't eaten themselves, then sleep until Sunday afternoon. But Julie had complained, and now I had to wait a full twenty-four hours from the time written on the box before eating. In a grand example of injustice, that time period still applied to the box of cheddar biscuits, which should be communal by default anyways.

I had argued that if we were transferring the role that a dish played on the table to its time in the fridge, then the cheddar biscuits should retain their communal properties. Julie said that normally this would be true, but since I can't resist eating all the cheddar biscuits in one shot, if I had missed the original meal that the biscuits were from, then I couldn't have access to the biscuits until the agreed upon twenty-four-hour period had passed and all the food becomes communal, which is fine by me, because when it comes to restaurant leftovers, I have the patience of a snake, and though I can't make it to work on time, at 8:49 tomorrow night, I will be pawing through the silverware drawer to find the perfect fork with which to poach my sister's scallops. You know what? I don't even need to eat anyway. I just spent an entire pool party with my arms crossed over my stomach and sweating so much that I could fill a bucket faster than a girl who saw me shirtless, and I don't need to gain any more weight before Naomi returns because even though I'm sure we're in love, I'm also sure that love has its limits.

When I open the door to my room, I'm surprised not to hear the clanking of empty soda cans pushed aside. I had cleaned my room yesterday and had decided that I was not going to drink soda tonight or any night until I got my weight under control. Usually on nights like this when I just had to beat the final boss, I would push soda cans up into my armpit like bullets pushed into a clip of a gun so I could carry them upstairs while still holding a chip bag or a carton of ice cream, then discharge the sugary slugs one after another into my blue-lit level-gaining face. I would drink them in what might be, at their shortest, fifteen-minute intervals—warm, cold, in a variety of flavors, a mad scientist who'll down any elixir in his all consuming quest to immunize himself against sexually transmitted diseases. I also, you know, pee in the soda cans sometimes instead of getting up to use the bathroom, and I almost circumcised myself on the surprisingly sharp mouth of the can when I glanced up to see my reflection in the game's loading screen and watched the teaser trailer for the most pathetic movie ever produced: *The Life and Times of Jacob Bigham.*

I mean, here's a concrete example of how much soda I drink. Last year Patrick Jungmo Kim, the exchange student from South Korea, was collecting soda can tabs because he heard they were made out of higher quality aluminum than the cans themselves and that this aluminum earned you more money when you turned it in because they made stuff like wheelchairs and airplane parts and crutches from them. A couple months after he asked for tabs, I brought in a whole Ziploc freezer bag stuffed with them. That same day James Reynolds walked up to Patrick and handed him his crutches, and I spent weeks obsessing over this perfect example of why James was who he was and why I am who I am. By turning in his aluminum, James declared himself healed a week early and limped onto the court to score twenty-four points; by turning in my aluminum, I was showing the world how I was drinking myself into immobility. I thought about putting this story into poem form and submitting it to the school paper after James's death, including a line with a pun about "his mettle and mine" but by that time I was beginning to have feelings for Naomi and I didn't want to try and impress her by eulogizing someone impossible to top. God I'm tired. Fuck a pool party.

I spend my entire time at work the next day as the sex-less liaison between the girls in concession and the male ushers who can actually perform specialized physical tasks. In the morning I am asked to find Lawrence so that he can take the film canisters upstairs to the projection booth. He is out front cleaning cigarette butts off the sidewalk, and when I ask about the canisters, I catch him glancing at my body and have to turn away, ashamed.

"Why didn't they ask you to do it?" asks Lawrence.

"You know why. It's because they think I'm too weak to lift them upstairs," I say because this is the closest I can get to confessing that I actually am too weak to lift them without actually saying it.

"Well are you?" asks Lawrence.

"Am I what?" I say.

"Are you too weak to lift them?" Lawrence asks, squeezing from my teats the warm drops of confidence that nurse in him the piglets of derision.

"Lawrence, I can lift one at a time, but you're the one they want so why not go?" I ask, motioning for his broom and dustpan. He hands them to me and I don't look at his face, but my hands still tingle at the smirk transference he's built up in the handle of the broom. In a single year I've had to love and hate two men whom Naomi chose to at least make out with, but soon I'll be the head of that pantheon and then we'll see who's smirking.

In the afternoon Mrs. Clemens has locked herself out of the office again, and I have to find Nate so that he can push aside the ceiling tiles and climb over the wall to drop into her office. Actually, I have to find Lawrence too so that he can give Nate a boost up because I had broken the step ladder during the first and only time I was allowed to attempt to change a lightbulb. Mrs. Clemens has already locked her keys in her office twice this summer, and every time Nate has to retrieve them, the entire staff gathers in the break room to watch him. Katrina in concession holds her hand over her mouth as she watches Nate's butt then shins then sneakers disappear into the ceiling, and the only sound we hear besides Nate's struggles across the mortarboard is the humming of the fluorescent lights. But it sounds like we're all humming, all concentrating to lend our savior energy as he ascends into the sterile sun to bargain for us the keys to heaven. And when he opens the red office door, the door to our hearts that we had within us all along, and we finally get a glimpse at the omniscience of the four-split screen of the security TV well, it's magical. I almost regret that this is my last day of work.

I guess washing our cars that evening counts as a work-out. I ran my truck through the wash on the way home so it would look clean, and I actually have to throw some dirt on it to make its condition match the crappy jobs I'm going to do on Mom, Julie, and Dad's cars. I can't believe that I also have to wash Dad's work truck, an old brown F100 with widely spaced Down syndrome headlights, every inch of its paint scabbed loose by tree limbs and the underlying rust ground together with spring pollen so that the corrosion looks alien and extreme, not the work of twenty years on Earth with us, but a single year abandoned on the oceanless beaches of Venus. I had just bought a new workout ensemble earlier today after work, and the green T-shirt's still stiff with newness and hasn't been sweated into enough to conform to the unwanted contours of my body, so I present a reasonably flat, unlumpy false front, a reflection I manipulate in the curve of the truck's now clean hubcaps until my chest is huge but my waist is thin, and I smile at my own funhouse physique to think that someday Naomi may be able to look past her upcoming love for my personality and see the body that I have prepared for her. Seriously though, school starts next week, and while I am not exactly where I need to be physically, I'm confident that Naomi will at least be able to see an improvement.

School begins with a chapel and an assembly, and I have to sit next to a new junior who hasn't learned enough about me to avoid me because Travis is in the AV booth with Kyle Marris, who's kind of head nerd at Stonewall and the leader of my social group. Sometimes I get to sit in the booth and read with a small flashlight and my back to the stage. But today, since I don't know how to do anything up there, when Travis heard my hands hit the rungs on the AV booth ladder, he slid open the panel to the booth and waved me away saying that "There's kind of a premium on space up here." So now I have to sit with the rest of my class and watch the ridges of Connor's product-daubed coxcomb rise above the back of his chair as he slouches through announcements. Where is Naomi? I do not see Naomi. I flip through the subjects on my Black Five Star notebook until I get to Naomi's section and read through the things I'd written about her over the summer to prepare for when we meet.

During the chapel Mr. Edens, the principal who this school insists on calling a headmaster, mentions the loss of James Reynolds. Jenny Briskin, our school's only visibly handicapped girl, bursts out crying in her wheelchair from the end of the senior aisle, and Mr. Edens has to descend from the stage to comfort her. Jenny is inconsolable, and Julie, who sits at the end of the aisle, nods when Mr. Edens asks her to wheel Jenny into the library. As they walk past, I wonder if I had died last year how loudly Julie would grieve for me.

I am the first one to make it to our table in the corner of the cafeteria, and while I'm not going to talk about cliques and shit, there's definitely a line of demarcation between the people who spent the beginning of their summer mod-chipping their PlayStations and those getting certified for CPR at the Y. I am taking small bites of my Pop Tarts and delicate sips of my Fruitopia because I read that you will eat less if you eat slowly. I'm also told you eat less if you keep a daily food diary, but fuck that; it would be like making daily additions to a suicide note if it ever fell into the hands of someone like Connor, who is currently shouting curses whenever one of his friends slaps an exposed sunburned shoulder peeking from beneath his sleeveless Big Johnson T-shirt. God, if Connor caught me writing down calories, my face would turn redder than that shoulder—that tight, not ripe, anti-evolutionary red that warns mates and attracts predators, the red I used to get after jogging laps to get a pity "C" in PE.

Lucas and Tommy and the other guys in our group have already sat down before Travis and Kyle arrive together, and Travis is carrying the briefcase with the projector in it, probably to project computer games on the wall of Kyle's bedroom after school while Travis sits in one of Kyle's two leather office chairs and rejoices at being able to be at the right hand of our school's nerd god.

Kyle is a shoo-in for salutatorian and is considered the smartest in the senior class because the valedictorian is a teacher's daughter. In addition to all the AV club stuff, he also makes the graphics and photo retouches for the school yearbook on his way better computer at home. After the bookstore's computer broke down, he was the only one who could recover all of the financial data, so the teachers pretty much let him have the run of the entire school. They gave him his own key to the computer lab, and they didn't say anything when he grew out his goatee. All the teachers are worried about who will take his place after he graduates. He and Travis are talking about tattoos.

"I'm saying there's no better idea for your first tattoo than to get the pattern of the sheets you lose your virginity on," Travis says. "That way it can be something memorable but also kind of random, and it comes with a great story."

"Yours is going to be cheap too," says Lucas. "Just a little white square from your time in prison. You can probably find some guy there to do it."

"I thought you would never admit you were still a virgin," says Kyle. "I thought all you talked about were girls."

This is bad for Travis because in the search for some provocative topic to bring up to Kyle, Travis forgot that he would divulge a detail about himself that would bring him under great scrutiny. Travis handles this well.

"I mean, I've done everything else besides that. Probably much more than you guys have and especially this past summer. I've gotten hand jobs, gotten blown, fingered a girl," and Travis is counting these acts out on his fingers as he says them and says "fingered" right as his left pointer finger touches his right middle finger.

"Ugh, OK, don't list them," says Kyle, and his look of disgust at Travis having to drag out his sexual résumé on the first day of school makes everyone at our table laugh.

""Bigham, seriously?" asks Travis. "Seriously, put that Pop Tart down for one sweet second and take a look at yourself. Think back to those times where you weren't eating or jerking off. There, you got those two or three points uploaded into your brain? Now, in any of these scenes do you ever see yourself even touching a girl? Not one. That's what I thought."

"Dude, I didn't say a goddamned thing, so don't attack me," I say. "Everybody laughed."

"I'm just saying the less you've done with a girl, the less you get to laugh, so you should be totally, completely silent," says Travis as if during homeroom this morning he sat through a PowerPoint presentation on ending embarrassing friendships. Now I've been singled out as the weakest guy at the weakest guy table in our school.

"Go fuck yourself, Travis," I say. "Then at least you'll be able to pick the sheets."

"At least someday I'll be fucking on sheets instead of wearing them," says Travis, spitting out the line of his life.

"Hey, can we not give Bigham a hard time about his weight this year?" asks Kyle. "I mean, he did lose some over the summer. Let's not discourage him." Now I know why Travis works so hard to impress him. "What tattoo would you get, Bigham?" asks Kyle.

"I don't know, a bear or a lion, I guess. Something that represents strength," I say.

"Pff...fat kids and strength," says Lucas, small red drops of baked-up blood flecking his freshly LASIKed eyeballs.

"Lucas, what did I just say, man?" asks Kyle.

"I'm just saying fat dudes always think they're stronger than normal and it's not true. Getting something that symbolizes strength inked on his body is like putting a fire exit sign on the surface of the sun."

"Lord God almighty," says Kyle. Tom Hammond whistles from the end of the table, takes out his pen, and begins writing on a napkin.

"Why am I being so owned?" I ask. "I didn't even insult anybody yet, and now I'm probably the most owned person at this school."

"Here you go, Lucas," says Tom Hammond and slides a napkin across the table at him that says my name on top, "property of" in the middle, and then Lucas's name below that with a line on the bottom of the napkin for Lucas to sign his name, which Lucas is doing right now. After signing the napkin, Lucas puts it in the front pocket of his new back-to-school golf shirt and smiles.

"Whoa whoa, you don't own everything Bigham yet," says Kyle. "You can't have his heart. Because this year it belongs to Naomi."

All the guys in our group had tried to go out with Naomi all through high school, and Kyle was the only one to achieve something resembling success, but that was when he was a freshman and I hadn't even met Naomi yet.

"How would you guys even know how I felt about Naomi?" I ask, looking toward Travis, wishing I had a tray to slam down instead of just a Pop Tart wrapper.

"It's fine, Bigham. Everybody here has fallen for her," says Kyle, sweeping his gaze over all the rival teams who've tried to plant a flag on Mount Naomi but have died ten miles below his base camp. "But you know that you'd have the least chance of any one of us, and we want to spare you what happened to Lucas."

At this Lucas has to wipe sudden tears away from his newly flattened corneas with the balled up deed to me.

"Guys, this is a really shitty way to treat me. Naomi's not even here, and I'm not going to do anything embarrassing. Also, fuck all of you."

There's five minutes left to lunch when Travis finally comes over to talk to me in the courtyard.

"Bigham, just come back to our table tomorrow, OK?" says Travis. "Don't pout for a week."

"How did you even know I had feelings for Naomi?" I ask. "I just told you that I had worked with her over the summer."

"In chapel we saw you open your notebook and there was a drawing of Naomi, and on the next page there were twelve lines of writing," Travis says. "Don't take that as a sign of your drawing talent, though. We wouldn't have been able to tell it was Naomi if you hadn't written 'Naomi' next to it."

"How did you see that all the way from the AV booth?" I ask.

"Lucas has better than 20/20 now," Travis says.

"That was one picture, Travis. One. And a single sonnet. I'm not going to show it to her or anything." I say.

"You've got one week until Naomi comes back, and we are trying to save you some embarrassment. You're going to be worse than Lucas, and he almost broke up the entire group. And now you're showing all the signs of being obsessed with her. You've got poems; you've got badly drawn Anime pictures of her staring at you from under a thin patina of your seed. It's the worst kind of crush, and you're going to go about it in the worst way," Travis says.

"Just because I'm the fattest here doesn't mean I don't at least get a shot," I say. "And it's not a shot, it's not. I'm allowed to be in love with her if that's what I think is going on."

"Fine, go ahead. Do everything middle-schooler wrong to her and see if she stays with this group for her whole senior year. Just don't flip out when she lets you down easy, and don't bring me into it."

"How could I bring you into it?" I ask. "But I won't."

"Naomi's done at this school anyway," says Travis. "No one's going to get to her, not after James died. He was an athlete and he died of a heart attack. Naomi's not going to get attached to a high risk guy like you."

Right now two football players have each grabbed an arm of Jenny Briskin's wheelchair and are grunting her up the stairs. James Reynolds used to be able to carry Jenny up by himself, chair and all, and Jenny got listed in the yearbook as "Assistant Physical Trainer" for weighing down James as he ascended the stairs, his calves flexing between taut coffee cake and sudden stone. James's dad was black and his mom was white, and the fact that he was handsome coupled with Stonewall's utter lack of diversity meant that James was a fixture on the school website's home page collage. After he died the school thought it might be inappropriate to have James's face still beaming from the center of the page as if he still attended, but they needed someone else to break up the utterly white array of faces, so the school's IT guy had scanned in a picture from a shoebox full of leftover yearbook photos of a black kid in a gray suit smiling gamely into the camera while sitting on one of Stonewall's signature blue benches. This kid was on the home page for three weeks until Naomi pointed out that he was in fact James's cousin, who had been at the memorial service for James that was held in our auditorium. The kid was removed immediately, but nothing says institutional regret like a hastily cropped collage. This is why Kyle is now in charge of the school's website.

"Travis, you haven't made fun of me like that since we were in like seventh grade," I say.

"Bigham, OK. I'm sorry, OK?"

"No, definitely not OK," I say.

"Just don't be another one of us who falls in love with her," Travis says. "Lucas fell way too hard last year, and Kyle gets mad at anyone who tries for her. She's the one girl who hangs out with us. It's kind of a huge cliché to go for her," Travis says. "Nobody's going to replace James, and I don't want you moping around after her all year embarrassing yourself."

"The only one embarrassing me is you!" I say. "I wasn't going to say anything about her in front of you guys. When Naomi comes back, you'll see just what is and what isn't a cliché," I say.

I have another week to get fitter for Naomi. Yes, I did lose some weight over the summer, and climbing the stairs to Algebra II is a lot easier for me now and I no longer make jokes about how I wish football players could carry me up on my wheelchair, but nothing really cosmetic has changed for me yet. I still look as fat as I was last year, and it's not like I can impress Naomi by showing her a readout of my blood pressure. I decide to start jogging. The dirt road beside my house usually doesn't have that many people who drive down it, but because of this, the people who do drive down it are not very careful. Besides, I cannot risk jogging in front of other people. I know that if a pickup truck flies by me on glittering wings of gravel dust and I hear the Doppler-stretched laughter of a passing detractor that I will curl into a little filled ditch and quit forever, my head pushed into the pink, rain-smoothed sand amidst the curled Styrofoam rinds of coffee cups, broken malt liquor bottles, and the rotting remains of poachéd does.

Our nearest neighbor, Mr. Sanders, has a pond not half a mile from his house. Sometimes he and Dad go down there to shoot bowling pins to splinters, but he said we could use his pond at any time. Mr. Sanders is a WWII veteran who fought in the actual Battle of the Bulge, so it's fitting that he's cleared the space in which I'll hold my own.

The only thing I remember from when they dug out the pond were the bulldozers that would wake me up on Saturday morning, grunting yellow mega fauna that circled each other in an ever-deepening ditch, preparing an elaborate nest in the middle of the wilderness but never mating, going suddenly extinct, their dream home filling up with dirty water. Through the years Mr. Sanders has alternately seeded the pond with the things that nourish and the things that injure: brim and buckshot, bread and bottle rockets, ducks and decoys. But these days the most he does is mow a path around the pond with his bush hog. It's that path that I can only make it around one and a half times before collapsing and having to sit on a shin-high pyramid of PVC pipe, the exposed bones of appropriated Southern forests. Two laps. I know I can make it for two laps before Naomi gets back. It's been an entire month since I've seen her, and I need to toughen up my heart so that it doesn't simply explode at the sight of her.

On Monday, the day Naomi returns, my heart does not in fact explode, but it comes close. I am the one who spots her first, the sun on the white concrete courtyard reflecting up and obscuring the finer features of her face between the black lace necklace and her newly short hair. She walks up to our pentagonal picnic table and picks the fifth I had occupied alone, setting her messenger bag between us. Well, this is it. She picked me. And the kicker is I'm prepared. I've worked with her, I've always been smart, and now I'm technically in the best shape of my life. I'm also in that sweet spot sexually, right between wanting to murder all women and wanting to become one myself. I am fully prepared to become Naomi's boyfriend.

"Hey guys, it's been a while," says Naomi, the words catching wetly in her mouth before shaking the constraints of her straight teeth and curling like newly minted pennies thrown into the twin mall wishing wells that are my ears.

"I can't believe you came back to America," says Kyle. "With all those Irish dudes slamming it to you."

"It wasn't Ireland, and you know that, Kyle," says Naomi. "Besides, I wouldn't trade you guys for all the dick in Scotland," says Naomi.

"Aww," says Kyle. "See that's why we love you, Naomi. You can hold your own with us."

"It's tough considering how you losers have been holding your own all summer," says Naomi, and then all the guys are doing their best Scottish brogues and talking about fucking her or something. I'm not listening. I'm thinking about those cleft photons spinning wildly in anticipation of finally becoming whole. Now they are less like photons and more like fireflies, buzzing on the right side of the mason jar of my brain, pushing my head toward hers, making her head lean toward mine, collecting in our temples, heating our cheeks. Help me, Naomi. Help me unite the light behind our eyes.

"But I did miss my boys," says Naomi. "Foreign dudes all think you're easy prey. I sure didn't miss working for Mrs. Clemens though, right Jacob?"

"Don't let Bigham talk to you," says Kyle. "You're just encouraging him to try and take it further."

"What? Am I hearing him right?" says Naomi, mock serious, turning halfway around in her seat, and putting her hand on my knee. "Well, Jacob had his chance all summer. We could have put a 'Do Not Disturb' sign on the stock room door and gone at it any time."

"Naomi, they have it all wrong," I say.

"What, you don't want to get with me?" laughs Naomi.

"No, I don't just want to have sex with you," I say, but the table erupts in incredulous *"Justs?"*

"Bigham, in addition to his regular garden-variety insatiable appetite, has developed one for love too," says Kyle. This is the cruelest I've ever seen him.

"Kyle, calm down. We agreed not to make those jokes anymore, not after last year," says Naomi.

"Naomi, we need a new official fat guy since Doug Hoffman moved last year and Bigham has been patiently waiting in the wings," says Kyle.

Travis boos and a couple other guys join in from around the table, and I'm glad they recognize that Kyle's gone out of bounds and he's not even trying to one-up me.

"Kyle. Quit it. Quit picking on him, and I'll talk to you later," says Naomi. "Right now I've got to talk to all my teachers and Mr. Edens about me missing the first week. You guys play nice."

She gets and walks into the main building, and I just sit there thinking how I'm the only one of us she mentioned by name on her first day back, except for Kyle, who she was yelling at.

"Kyle," says Travis. "You know if Bigham was going to say something about being in love with her he would have done it, but no he shut up. And you fired off like three jokes about him being fat with no provocation."

"We're going to lose Naomi for another year if you keep talking like that," says Lucas.

"Yeah," says Travis. "She spent the summer before avoiding Lucas, last year dating James, and this summer getting over his death. And you hit Bigham because he's just starting to get his crush on like every one of us has."

"Bigham, I'm sorry, man," says Kyle. He's staring at his nails, furious with himself. "This is the first time I've gotten to talk to her in a long time. Plus, she blocked me on IM during the summer. I'm mad when she talks to anyone. I just took it out on you. Maybe you should go to another group where you'll just be punched if another guy is jealous."

"It's OK, Kyle. I'm not mad." I can't possibly be mad after she touched my knee. I'm not even mad at my sudden erection that shot down the left side of my fly and actually thankful for the gut that covered it. I didn't even think I could get an erection around Naomi with how intensely I felt thinking about her getting in the way. Maybe that happens with every girl who touches you and not just Naomi, but it's good to have that sort of evolutionary fail-safe should we eventually try to have sex. If we fall in love, I guess I should try to look at sex as a sort of blessed inevitability, as natural a reaction as my boner.

Every afternoon for the next two weeks I jog laps around the pond. When Westvaco cleared out space for the pond, they left a single, ostracized sassafras standing close to where the path around the pond begins. I start each exercise session by leaning against this tree for balance, splaying my hand over the thin metal NO TRESPASSING sign nailed around its upper trunk, and reaching back to grab my shoe with my other hand. I'm so weak and unbalanced that it takes me a couple tries to grab my own foot, like trying to shoe the skittish colt that is myself, until finally I manage to crack the loaf of artisan bread of my leg into a dimpled knee. I can make it three laps around the pond before trying to literally eat the air—all of it, the entire troposphere. Today it is raining hard, and I decide to try and jog up the path back to my house to get out of the rain quicker, the water beating the red clay until it eddies into orange foam that splashes past my sneakers. Dad is smoking his pipe on the porch, sitting on a scavenged church pew, its varnish cracked and flaking like the skin on chapped lips.

"Out jogging even in the rain?" Dad asks. "That's good, even though you did get your shoes soaked with dinosaur puke."

"Dinosaur what?" I say, leaning to catch my breath against the birthday pillar, where Julie and I stood to get our heights marked with a Sharpie every year. I am staring at "Jacob—13", which is right at eye level, even though I am barely leaning over. Eye level. I was counting on that growth spurt to make me thin.

"You don't remember that even when you were five years old you could remember all the ways the dinosaurs might have died?" Dad asks.

I kind of remember, but I can't concentrate because I've been too busy trying to burn all the excess calories causing my own singular extinction. However, I make that little extra effort and try to talk to my father.

"Yeah, I talked about the comet, and how small mammals might have eaten all their eggs, or maybe an ice age or an epidemic might have killed them all."

"Yeah, they got sick. All the biggest animals ever to walk the earth getting sick at the same time. That's what I told you that foam was. All their fossilized barf," he says, whisking me back to an age more antiquated than the Cretaceous, a time when I took whatever he said seriously.

"Oh yeah, I remember. That was pretty gross," I say.

"Well, Mom's going to be home late tonight. She's got a meeting. But I am making spaghetti," Dad says, getting up to knock the ashes from his pipe against another pillar and watching them sizzle against a curtain of rain pouring from the roof.

"OK, thanks," I say, and go inside, but after I slap my soaked clothes into the hamper to lie for a minute on my bed, I fall asleep naked and wake up hungry. It's late, and the downstairs TV is off, so I walk down in just my boxers. On top of the breadbox is a bag of fun-size Snickers that I immediately tear into but stop before eating the first one. Instead, I take the bag outside with me onto the front porch and begin to unwrap the bars, one by one, and fling them into the dark, wet forest. Every time I throw a bar, the flab on my upper arm reverberates; I want to throw junk food into the forest every night until my body no longer reacts to the effort. I'm down to the last bar, but it smells so much like chocolate that it's almost impossible to let fly. I hold it between my thumb and forefinger, tempted against the throw, holding it for so long that a tendril of melted chocolate begins to snake across my palm. Each bar already bears my thumbprint on its chocolate, but for this last one my thumb has almost bored into the nougat. I finally manage to throw every bar of candy away. Instead of standing on my front porch in my boxers, I might as well be in my underwear in front of homeroom—I'm just as out of breath, embarrassed, and surrounded by little snickers. This Tuesday I will call Naomi.

I don't talk with Naomi at all on Monday. I can't talk with her, actually, because I'm so nervous about talking to her that I licked my lips all Monday, and now they are chapped and swollen, but she won't be able to see that over the phone, and maybe over the course of our conversation, I'll be able to quickly switch the receiver from my ear to my lips and have the vibrations of her voice speed their healing. I don't really mean that, by the way. I'm not that obsessed. Tuesday she calls out sick, so now I have an excuse to call her tonight and see if she's OK.

On Tuesday afternoon I jog so hard while thinking about Naomi that I don't realize how tired I am until I'm dou-bled over and layering thin skeins of vaguely orange puke over the cicada skin of my lips and into a ditch beside the pond, proving that prehistoric puke is, in fact, a renewable resource.

That night I wait until nine when Mom and Dad are asleep before calling Naomi. I almost never talk to people over the phone, except for thanking the grandparents for Christmas gifts, or sometimes Travis calls and tells me to come over. Julie is on the computer right next to where the phone is, and I have to warn her that I'm coming over so she has time to minimize all her IM windows like I give a damn who she's talking to or know their screen names anyway. I take the phone from its cradle and Julie asks, "Who are *you* about to call?"

I don't even answer her, I just go straight upstairs. I have to call Naomi while I'm standing up. I can't do it like Travis, lying back in his beanbag chair and teasing girls about how their hair looked that day. Sometimes I think Travis has me over just to watch him talk to girls. I don't know Naomi's cell number and have to look her home number up in the school's student/teacher directory. I wait until 9:12, to make it look spontaneous. When I call an older woman's voice picks up and asks who it is.

"Hello, Mrs. Naomi. This is Jacob Bigham. May I please speak to Naomi?"

"Mrs. Who?" Naomi's mother asks.

"Mrs. ummm...McKenzie, I know Naomi from school. Can I speak to her? Is she there?" At this point I'm grateful that the word "ummm" ends with the first letter of Naomi's last name. Otherwise I would never have remembered.

"Yeah, sure, Jack, let me go get her," she says, and while she's gone I hold the receiver away from my mouth so I can breathe as loudly as I want for a few precious seconds.

"Hey, I don't know who this is," says Naomi into her phone. "I don't know a Jack."

"You don't know Jack!" I say, trying to laugh afterward.

"No, I mean I don't think I've ever talked to anybody named Jack," says Naomi.

"Oh, your mom heard me wrong. This is Jacob from Stonewall."

- 67 -

"I know where you're from, Jacob," says Naomi, saying my name. Being playful. "Why did you call?"

"Well, you weren't at school today, and I thought you might be sick," I say.

"Nope, just taking the day off," Naomi says. "I know I shouldn't after missing a week at school because of my trip, but I've been just exhausted. But that was sweet that you thought to call."

"We thought you might be coming down with some of that mad cow disease they had over there in Scotland or something, "I say.

"Oh man, that is so sad. I read about that the other day online. Did you see that picture of that pile of lambs being bulldozed into a ditch?" Naomi asks.

"No, but that image contains such a shocking dichotomy. Lambs and bulldozers. Not quite like fire and ice, but, you know, something small and soft like a lamb and then that big old bulldozer," I say.

"Right, I get it. That's a good word for it, dichotomy," she says.

"I knew you'd get it," I say. "That's why you hang out with us, you know, the smart guys. Just throwing these words around."

"Uh-huh," she says. "So, yeah, I was just absent today. Definitely gotta watch those. They let me slide sometimes and do make-up work, but you know." I hear a few low notes over the phone.

"What's that sound?" I ask.

"I'm just messing around with the piano," she says.

"Can you not do that for a while?" I ask. "I'm calling to try to tell you something." I say.

"Oh, OK. Sorry. What is it you wanted to tell me?" Naomi asks.

"Well, I called to say that I've weighed the evidence and that I'm in love with you," I say, feeling my breath collect in the grooves of the receiver. "I really am. I've liked girls before and thought about them a lot. But I think about you all the time. I wanted to tell you that the first time I called so that I wouldn't waste your time." I will stop breathing for as long as it takes for her to respond, but now all I can hear is Naomi breathing through her button nose, and I grow envious of her breath, the way it gets to fill her chest then blow out over her breasts. The receiver begins to smell like baby powder.

"Jacob, babe, you're not in love with me. I mean, that's sweet of you to call and all, but I've handled this before and with our group. You've just got a crush on me," she says. "I mean, it's happened to both Lucas and Kyle, and now it's happening with you. It's OK, it happens. I'm probably the only girl you hang out with and we get along, but I just don't think we'd work out."

Maybe part of what I like about Naomi is her need to initially resist the inevitable, but I am alone in love and hate waiting for her here.

"Naomi, this is different than having a crush. This is like being crushed," I say. "I know that I could never be as good as James but—"

"We're not talking about him," says Naomi.

"I'm sorry, but it's not just because you're in the group. I would feel this way even if you were outside of the group."

"Other groups trade around their girls and guys, and everybody gets too mad to stay together, except when they're drunk at parties," she says. "And in any other group with girls like me, I'm sure you'd have your shot with plenty of them more your speed."

"Naomi, I've never been drunk and there's no more room in me for other girls anymore. And you're my speed, you know? You're my speed." I tried to sound older when I called her, but now my voice is getting higher.

"Don't worry, babe," she says. "Just don't get upset. It's so bad when guys get upset over the phone. You should know that for next time. I mean, first of all, you don't know anything about me."

"I know enough, Naomi," I say, and I shouldn't be this mad hearing her voice. There was a certain point in the conversation that everything after the word "just" frustrated me.

"Enough?" she asks. "Name a band I like or something, anything."

"I know as much as any guy at school. Plus, I hate hearing people list out bands like it defines exactly who they are, and their eyes dart around after every band name looking for approval but they're too busy saying the next band." I inhale. "Not you. But other people at parties."

"Jesus," she says.

"Listen, I'm sorry. I didn't know that it would go this badly with you." Instead of letting her hear me start to cry I rasp the receiver underneath my doubled, stubbled chin and wish it were the barrel of my father's shotgun.

"What was that?" asks Naomi.

"Sorry, I dropped the phone for a second," I say, apologizing again.

"Calm down, Jacob. OK? You have to know that you just can't call and tell someone you're in love with them. Now, you're one of my guys and you don't have a lot of experience with girls, so we can just let this all go."

"It's my weight, isn't it?" I ask.

"It isn't anything," she says.

"Naomi, I—"

"I'm going to hang up now, Jacob. You need to stop crying, settle down, and get your head together."

When I wake up the next morning, I hear both the phone ringing into my chest and Dad downstairs yelling about the whereabouts of the aforementioned phone. By the time I hand the phone to him, the answering machine is already playing the message from the wife of Dad's substitute for the mail route, telling Dad how Jim couldn't make it to work because he's had a heart attack this morning, just a little one.

Dad takes the phone from me and tells tells Jim's wife that he understands that it's a hell of a man who thinks about work when he's having a heart attack and he hopes that Jim makes it through OK.

"What were you doing with the phone, Jacob, talking your girlfriend to sleep?" asks Dad.

"Yeah, something like that," I say.

"All right, I knew it."

Over the next few days, I keep a pretty low profile at Stonewall, taking two nectarines and half a packet of imitation crabmeat with me to eat on the concrete bleachers behind the baseball field. Mom and Dad don't comment about what food I choose to get when I go with them to the grocery store. They knew that I am trying a weird diet when instead of Friday night pizza I ate a one serving can of microwaveable beef stew. Later that night I did go downstairs and eat all the sausage off of two leftover slices but fed the rest of the pieces to Honey, our dog.

Every day I run through why I cried to Naomi over the phone and what it might mean for me and her. I just don't think that I'm used to saying anything emotional to her. To her credit, Naomi took it well. She waved hi to me in the hallway on the following day, and I know she hasn't told anybody because Travis would be making fun of me.

In third grade our class was sitting Indian-style in a sharing circle while Mrs. Johnson read us a parable about an old man and a bet between the Sun and the North Wind. Apparently the North Wind and the Sun had been feuding all day over who was more powerful, and so the Sun dared the North Wind to set a challenge that would settle who was the greater natural phenomenon.

"At that point, the Sun spied an old man walking along the path," said Mrs. Johnson, catching a page of the book on one of the wooden buttons holding together the denim dress stretched across her breasts. "And the Sun said, 'Whomever makes that man take off his coat is more powerful,'" continued Mrs. Johnson, looking up from the book to see me digging wet red clay from between the treads of my sneakers with the end of a pencil and placing the curled-up pieces of dirt, like giant cinnamon shavings, into the trash can beside me.

"Jacob, are you paying attention?" she asked.

"The Sun and the North Wind are about to have a contest to see who is the most powerful," I say.

"Yes," said Mrs. Johnson, pausing to purse her lips bitterly at having been beaten in a judo bout of academic dynamics. By summarizing the story, I proved that not only did I know where exactly we were, but then she had no option other than to agree with me. She couldn't reprimand me because I couldn't have paid better attention to her if I had been staring her straight in the face.

"Now the North Wind began to gently blow against the old man at first. But this only made the old man button all his buttons. The North Wind got frustrated and began to blow harder, but this only made the man hold his coat tightly. Finally, the North Wind got so angry that he blew as hard as he could…whoooooosh," said Mrs. Johnson, turning to blow a few stray strands of straw-colored hair from Marcus Blaymire's forehead, causing him to giggle, and also caus-ing him years later to be caught by his sister in their home's computer room jerking off in front of an oscillating fan.

"But the man just held his coat as tightly as possible, even with the wind whipping around him, and the North Wind had to give up. 'Fine!' said the North Wind to the Sun, 'Let's see if you can make him take his coat off.'"

"The Sun smiled and slowly began to grow brighter, gently warming the man, until the man cheerily began to unbutton his coat and sling it over his shoulder, whistling as he walked along the road," said Mrs. Johnson. "This story teaches us that in order for us to get what we want, it's bet-ter for us to be nice and gentle like the Sun, instead of mean and pushy like the North Wind."

"That doesn't make sense," I said.

"Why not?" asked Mrs. Johnson, crisply dog-earing the page of follow-up questions before closing the storybook.

"The Sun wasn't doing anything nice or special; it was just doing what it always does. The wind just made a stupid bet," I said.

"No, the Sun was being patient and warm toward the man, and the man responded by doing what the Sun wanted. But the North Wind was being mean, and the man responded by refusing to do what the North Wind wanted," said Mrs. Johnson.

"No, because if the Sun had been just as mean as the Wind, then the man would still have taken his coat off just because it's the Sun. The Sun is warm," I said.

"Yes, I know the Sun is warm," said Mrs. Johnson, using her breath to pff up the wisps of hair that comprise the fringe women pull over the tops of their skulls when they wear the rest of their hair in a ponytail.

"Like there was no way the Wind could have won that bet anyway," I said. "The man already started off with his coat on. Even if the Wind had been nice and just made it a little cooler, the man would have still kept his coat on."

"Jacob, let's pretend that the Sun and the North Wind are people," said Mrs. Johnson.

"Like if the bet had been who could make the man put his coat on, then the Wind could be as mean or nice as he wanted, it doesn't matter. People can act in different ways, but the Sun is always going to be warm, and the Wind is always going to be cold. And if both were as mean as possible, that man wouldn't have had a chance. Like the Wind could have ripped him apart, or the Sun could have burned the jacket off him," I said. "Hugo blew down our pool; the North Wind was actually holding back for this man."

"Jacob, right now you are being like the Wind. You're just trying to bowl me over so I can't fight back," said Mrs. Johnson. "But see now, I am going to be like the Sun and let out class a little early so you all can go out and be with the real sun," said Mrs. Johnson.

But that afternoon she sent a note home with me to give to my parents about me being uncooperative in class, which I threw out our car window as Mom drove us home and let the North Wind carry it to wherever he buries arrows aimed against his allies. I thought for a long time after that, "This is bullshit. The third grade is bullshit."

But I guess Aesop and, by association, his modern-day acolyte Mrs. Johnson have a point in that oftentimes the gentleness or severity of our endeavors doesn't matter; it is only our basic nature that affects the results. This is why James Reynolds could succeed with Naomi and not me. Both of us are powerful entities in our own right, but only one has managed to get Naomi to take her clothes off. Because no matter what James did, Naomi would have been attracted to him because he was warm and radiant like the sun, whereas no matter how hard I try to impress her, Naomi will always get the sick shivers thinking about me kissing her because I am like the wind, and I totally blow. In order to get Naomi, I can't just intensify my already unsuccessful methods. This will only make me more of an intense loser. Rather, I will have to change my very nature to be like James Reynolds.

On Friday afternoon I start pressing sections of telephone poles above my head in an effort to be more rugged. Years ago Dad had hauled home scrap telephone poles and chainsawed them into four-foot sections so that he could half bury them down our driveway in an effort to combat erosion. Since we live on the second highest spot in our county, after every rain there'd be a large red crescent of sand washed out of our driveway and across the asphalt. So Dad figured that alternating telephone poles would help to terrace our driveway and keep it from completely washing away in the summer thunderstorms.

At first Dad had wanted me to help him cut the poles, but I could barely lift one end on top of the sawbuck. It was almost too difficult to even bend down that low to grip them, so I just put my hands on both sides of the pole and waited for him to do the real lifting, but sometimes, in sympathy, I had grunted. Before cutting the first pole into sections, he had to remove a thick wire of copper, corroded to a bright green, which ran down the spine of each pole. The wire was held in place by industrial staples so strong they looked like double-ended nails bent in half, but after Dad pulled out the first one in two easy twists, I prepared to hear him extol the virtue of Vise-Grips:

"Goddamn, these things are great. Vise-Grips are one of those things you're sure somebody got rich off of but you don't mind because they deserved it. Every one I buy is like a little silver hand that never lets go till I tell it to."

The staples were inches deep in the stubborn wood, and I could hear the wood crackle as Dad pried them out from around the wire. Dad flipped each staple into the crotch of the sawbuck; it looked so much like he was pulling out an entire row of wisdom teeth, the way he wrenched them from the wood and put them to the side, each staple's roots curved back and overlong, crusty with bloody rust. "Here, Jacob, you try yanking out one of these suckers."

He handed me the Vise-Grips across the pole, and I saw him through my fogged goggles, the ones he always made me wear whenever he was about to chainsaw something. It took me a couple tries and both hands to even clamp the Vise-Grips down in the middle of the staple, and even after straining with my entire body and letting out about a dozen trapped piglet sniffles, I couldn't get the staple out.

"Don't try to yank upward, Jacob. Press down and use the tool as a lever. C'mon, it's not that hard. You can do it,"

Dad said. But I knew I couldn't; I could sense right after I gave that first yank of kid strength. I knew that the sides of my back didn't expand like his, that my sneakered feet scrabbled around on the ground trying to find purchase in the wood chips and didn't land with the deliberate weight of his rough boots. "Hey, now you got to be able to do this," said Dad, his expectant voice resting on the top of my head, the voice that he can only correctly perform if he puts his hands on his hip. "Just use your weight." After hearing him say that, I just let go of the Vise-Grips and stalked off toward the house. "Jacob. Jacob. I didn't mean it like that. I wasn't thinking," Dad shouted at my back, over my exaggerated stomps up the steps. This was a year and a half ago, and he hasn't suggested that I help him out in any of his projects since, partly I think over guilt about letting me know he knew I was fat, and partly because I wouldn't be able to help out at all.

But now I can lift one of these sections over my head for three times in a row, although on the last repetition I had to pause with the center of the pole balanced on my forehead, and the creosote still coating the pole caused me to rip a pale corn silk forelock of my own hair out of my head once my elbows extended, and, though I had originally planned to yell only out of effort, an additional, genuine yelp of pain came after it like an undiscovered, stunted and deformed twin sliding out after the baby you've already named.

That night while tweezering ticks off of Honey, I take one that I find near her ears and with Dad's flashlight I go outside to find the section of the pole that has my hair and bits of my scalp stuck to shiny brown bubbles of creosote and press the still-struggling tick into the pitch, right next to my hair, so that in the future they can clone me and my dog from preserved bits of telephone pole amber. This will have to do until lifting the poles above my head enables me to preserve my genetics through more traditional means.

CHAPTER 5

Classes are going fine. Not Mom and Dad deflector "fine," but they're going OK and that's nothing new. I've never had any trouble with school. Today I brought all my CDs in a little CD carrier in my book bag. I don't have nearly as much music as my friends and especially my sister because she's got a ton of CDs and just bought her second CD stacker yesterday. This CD carrier isn't even mine; it's one that Julie had thrown away and that I had salvaged from the trash.

Computer science is the only class I have with Travis, since he doesn't give half a damn about getting into other advanced classes but he really knows his stuff about computers. This is why I need to talk to him today about the CDs because he's got a much nicer computer than ours at his house. In class I stop working on my spreadsheet and hand the case to Travis, who's sitting next to me in the ring of computers that surround our desks.

"Travis, I need you to make a compilation CD for me, please."

"Why do you need one, Bigham?" asks Travis, who quickly pauses and minimizes his game of *Chrono Trigger*, not because he's worried about getting caught by Mr. Jefferson, who's constantly out of the room taking care of all the computers in the entire school, but because he's working on his fastest run-through of every one of the game's thirteen possible endings and has just started on the eighth.

"Bigham, look, I just started, and look, I named Chrono after you. Guess who I'm naming Marle after? Is there enough room? Yes, there is. N-A-O-M-I," Travis says, entering each letter as he says them.

"Quit it, Travis, please," I say, wondering if he knows that every time I get to name a love interest in a video game I always name her Naomi. "Naming your characters is just going to slow your time."

"Shit," says Travis as he reloads a previous save state. "Besides, why do you need me to make you a CD anyway?" asks Travis. "It's not like you have a huge library. All you have is like ten CDs of movie soundtracks."

"They're more like cinematic scores, Travis," I say. "Like symphonies and stuff and themes, not just thirteen songs that were popular two months before the movie came out."

"Yeah, OK, it's all classical," says Travis.

"Orchestral more like. Or, I guess, symphonic. Classical's a period of music, it's actually incorrect to apply that term to anything that has an orchestra."

"Bigham, I had to tell you who The Clash was. Even when you're asking me for a favor you're correcting every single thing I say."

"I'm sorry, Travis. It's just that I've been working out a lot lately, and I've kind of plateaued. I need like a whole sixty-minute program so that I can keep going without having to change CDs."

I'm not afraid of talking about working out in the middle of class because everybody else is screwing around, changing the screensavers so that passing students can know that Stonewall sucks, or raiding Mr. Jefferson's desk for paper clips and rubber bands, or downloading Instant Messenger again like every day before it's wiped away when the computers are put to sleep for the night.

I hand Travis the case, and inside is a four-folded piece of notebook paper torn from my journal. This paper is something I'd want nobody else to see, because it may be the most pathetic scrap of paper in the entire world, more pathetic than the little yellow Post-It note Mom stuck onto the top of the butcher block in our kitchen last year saying, "Jacob, don't eat the dinner rolls or the chips. They are for company," and narrowly edging out the orange piece of construction paper I had passed to Mrs. Johnson that read "I have pooped myself please call my parents." It's actually a handwritten track list for a mix CD for Naomi, and on this paper are the songs that, when I listen to them, they bring me close to feeling like I do when I think about her, and if she listens to it in the order I've put down, I'm sure it'll nudge her toward the same wavelength.

Naomi's been so withdrawn lately. She hardly ever sits at our table, and when she does she barely talks. She never smiles. In between doing her Spanish homework she just holds her pen with the pink fluffball on the end in front of a nascent zit. When we sit across from each other at the pentagonal picnic table in the courtyard, I can hear the clink of her firefly mind rushing to the front of her forehead. She's thinking about me. She wants all the things that make up us, all the thoughts buzzing and briefly bioluminescent to be poured into the larger jar that is my newly Febrezed and crumb-free bed.

"OK, Bigham, anything to help you out," Travis says. "I mean, I don't hear you breathing over the computer fans when you sit next to me in class, so I think you're making some sort of progress."

"Thanks a lot, man," I say.

"No, I mean I'm serious," says Travis, stuffing the CD case into his JanSport. I can tell that you're improving. And you should quit moping in the gym at lunch and hang with us again. You don't even have to be afraid of having to deal with Naomi. She doesn't even sit with us anymore. She sits with her girlfriends in the cafeteria. She talks with your sister more than she talks with us. Maybe that's why you're losing weight. You were afraid of eating in front of her."

"You wait and see, Travis," I say. "It's happening to her, I think. Her leaving just proves that she's thinking through something big and needs to be away from us."

"Have you even tried to talk her lately?" asks Travis.

"Yeah, on the phone a couple of times," I say.

"At least you're not trying to talk with her at the table anymore. Jeez, that made everybody uncomfortable, and I'm never going to let you forget it. Do you remember it?"

"Yes, I remember it," I say, looking back at my book on how to use Excel and trying to divine the financial future of Company XYZ.

"You really, really remember how embarrassing that was, and you don't need me to remind you?" asks Travis. "Huuuuuuhhhhhhh?"

"Yes, I screwed up that day in front of the guys, and I remember how everybody else kind of looked away except for you. You know that feeling when you're about to get the flu? I had that feeling except it had to do with Naomi, and if I hadn't called her beautiful right then, I felt like I would have gone home sick."

"Well, you made us all sick that day, Bigham. As I recall, you called her, and I'm quoting you now—do you hear me preparing to quote you? You said, 'Naomi, you are soul-annihilatingly beautiful today.' I liked how she made you repeat it. That's the best part."

"She didn't make me repeat it. She just didn't hear it right the first time," I say, reaching over quickly and hitting the button that ejects his project floppy and tossing it over my shoulder so that it clatters across the tops of the empty desks behind us, like a skipping stone. But Travis doesn't care. He's back to his game and still laughing to himself.

"Sure, I'll get you your CD, Bigham," he says. "Anything to make you better than what you are now."

Julie's still driving me home because Dad thinks it's a waste to have two cars from the same family drive to school every day, but it's still humiliating, especially because she treats me like a burden, like instead of being just one grade behind her I go to a special school that sits adjacent to Stonewall. Julie's actually got a study hall scheduled for her last class, and sometimes she'll drive off at two o'clock to drink shakes at Sonic with her other senior friends and not come back until half an hour after school lets out. That's what she did today, and when she finally pulled up around to the front of the school where I sat on the steps, she just stayed in the car, pop music shaking the panes, and motioned for me to get in.

We spend the entire drive home not talking to each other, which is not unusual. I just sit there chewing gum, trying not to screech at Julie for stranding me there at school while she's off being popular. Chewing gum causes me not to think about food, and it's also part of a program to help hone my masculine reactions, like silence. This gum, this white spearmint grub, this greatly exaggerated fat cell, is being crushed by the only muscles that I can make bulge, my jaw muscles, my masseters, the only muscles tough enough to recognizably survive a fire.

"Masseters—more like mass eaters!" Connor would say if he was smarter and could also read my thoughts. Instead of arguing with Julie, I just sit there staring out the window and think of Naomi receiving my CD, of the guaranteed forty-two minutes that I'll have in her mind. There'll be some pretty epic tracks on there, some doozies that synch up with how strongly I feel about Naomi whenever the orchestra kind of climaxes.

Travis hands me the CD on Friday in computer science, but he's already written "Big Ham's Muscle Mix" on it in black marker.

"Travis, c'mon now, you wrote on it!" I say.

"So?" says Travis. "You need it labeled so it doesn't get lost in that huge nine-CD library. Once you break that one-digit barrier, things can get out of hand."

I'm already walking over to Mr. Jefferson's desk, and I can hear the entire class shutting up because they know I'm Mr. Good Student and they think I'm going over to press the secret call button under his desk that sets off bad-behavior klaxons across the entire upper school. I find a black Sharpie marker in the desk drawer and walk back to my computer.

"Yeah, but I don't want my dad to know that I'm making all these plans to get buff," I say, painstakingly scribbling a solid black rectangle over Travis's writing.

"Why? What does it matter if your dad knows?" asks Travis.

"You know when you first declare to your family that you're starting a big project, and they encourage you at first, but you're afraid that they'll keep bringing it up way past the time when you've already given up on it?" I ask.

"Yeah," says Travis. "One time my dad saw me messing around with his guitar and tried talking to me about it, but afterward I just put it down forever. I mean, trying to do something that your dad's already good at is the most nerve-racking thing ever. It's never worth it."

"Yeah. I mean, my dad starts learning that I'm trying to get fit, he'll want to hold the punching bag for me or whatever sitcom shit he thinks up," I say, still marking on the CD. I decide to color the whole thing black. I don't want Naomi to think that this CD was originally meant for someone else.

"Well, if it's that bad, I can just make you another copy. Those things are pretty cheap. Let me toss that one at Jessica's boyfriend over there. She'll think it's hilarious," he says.

"No, I'll lose a whole weekend if we do that. I need some inspiration to get me back on track," I say, and now the CD doesn't look so bad, if I'm careful coloring it all in—kind of glossy, less generic than just a plain old CD.

After school gets out, I wait outside in the front parking lot, a couple spaces away from Naomi's, under one of the trees planted in its concrete square, because even this late in the year it's still hot if you stand for a while in direct sunlight. I want the last image she has of me before she plays the CD to be a good one, not me squinting at her with my under-arms ringed with sweat, not having the damp of my palms make that little sweat squeak when I pass the CD's jewel case from my hand to hers. For once I'm glad that Julie's out with her friends again in town so she won't be beeping at me from across the parking lot during the exchange.

I see Naomi walking down the pathway between the main building of the school and the gym, the sleeves of her black sweatshirt tied around her hips, her midriff show-ing. Midriffs aren't allowed at Stonewall, so the girls just wear sweatshirts through the cool morning and the air-con-ditioned afternoon, and as soon as the last class gets out, they take off the sweatshirt. She's got green canvas pants on and sneakers, and the white T-shirt has some Japanese character on it. I remind myself not to stare at her belly but-ton. I resolve not to look at her boobs. The entire torso is written off for looking at. She's just chucking her messenger bag of books into the passenger seat of her car and waving good-bye to a couple of her girlfriends when I walk up behind her.

"Hey, Naomi," I say while her back is turned, knowing that she's about to get in the car and I don't want her to have already sat down.

Naomi turns around.

"Oh, hey, Jacob," she says, shielding her eyes against the afternoon sun. "You doing better? I mean, are you doing OK, after the phone call?"

"Oh yeah. I guess I got a little too worked up, you know. But I'm fine now. I have a CD for you to listen to," I say, holding out the case.

"Thanks," she says, taking the case and looking down at it, then turning it over to look at the back. "Who is it?"

"It's from a band I think you'll like, Dump Truck Full of Lambs."

She looks up from the CD at me, uncomprehending.

"I meant bulldozer," I say, and her jaw sort of moves to the side as she looks at me, her eyes wider but still squinting. Gosh, so cute. I read somewhere that there was actually a mathematical system to determine the attractiveness of a face, all having to do with that face's balance and symmetry, but to me a girl is most cute when that initial symmetry is briefly disturbed by something, whether by puzzlement, or by laughter, or by concentration.

"From when we were talking on the phone about your time in Scotland," I say. "Anyway, it's not really one band, it's a compilation, and I think it explains a lot of things, you know, about how I feel."

"OK," she says. "Right! On the phone about the lambs. Well, I've got to get on home now. I've got a CD player right here in the car so I can listen to it on the way, all right, Jacob? Thanks, I'll give it back to you Monday."

"No, you can keep it. It's yours. And maybe you should wait until you get home to listen to it, you know?" I don't want her to get overwhelmed and lose control of the car.

"Right, sure," she says, getting into her car. "I'll see you again tomorrow. On Monday, I mean." She closes the door and gives me a little wave from behind the window, and I give a little wave back.

On Monday afternoon after school I'm shooting jump shots in the gym, not really jump shots yet, more up-on-my-tiptoe shots, waiting for Julie to come in and wave me to her across the gym so she can silently drive me home.

"Bigham, man."

It's Travis. Usually we joke around for a few minutes after our last class and then his mom drives him home, but today he's sought me out. He just stands there with his arms folded around his chest, a coach's posture, like he's about to let a whistle drop from his lips and critique my technique. In the middle of the gymnasium someone like Travis—with his thin build and mass of curly hair—looks like a black flower blooming in the desert. Travis is standing on the school seal right where James Reynolds had a heart attack and died, and he reminds me of a flower that can only bloom in the desert if it snakes from the putrefying eye socket of a freshly collapsed camel. Not like I'm comparing James to a camel, it just appears that in this gym, with championship flags hanging from the rafters from the years when James played, it's like someone like me or Travis can only briefly survive in this harsh environment if we take nutrients from the rotting body of a much greater physical being.

"What is it, Travis? You look disappointed. I know how to shoot," I say, getting ready to take another shot, this time hoping he sees me make it. That specific hope keeps me from making this shot, and the ball smacks against the backboard.

"You didn't tell me that that CD you made me make was for Naomi," says Travis, arms still folded, looking down and toeing the edge of the court with the same sandals he wears every day, even the single day it snowed an inch last year, one additional inch away from paralyzing every high school in the state .

"I'm sorry. It's even more embarrassing for me to talk about being kinda in love with Naomi than me trying to get in better shape," I say, jogging after the ball. "I'm making progress in both, though. Total progress. Measurable. With goals."

"Yeah, well, you know Naomi's in that English 101 class, right? And they have to read out of their journals every class?" Travis asks.

"The one they run through the college, yeah. Well, we don't make dumb friends. All the guys are in that class too," I say. I line up another shot from the foul line, take it, and make it. "So she read a journal entry about me making the CD for her in class, right? I guess it's good that everybody knows."

Travis inhales like he's been trying to teach me how to tie my shoes for the past half hour. For a frayed-jean fuck-up he's getting awfully patronizing.

"Yeah, Bigham? Yeah? Well, when she read about how you gave her this black CD that had the *Star Wars* theme and the *Superman* theme on it. Plus some song about Nazis."

I stand with the ball in my hands, and I start turning it over and over again, like I'm trying to smooth it out.

"I don't get this," I say, not getting it. "I didn't ask for any of those songs on there."

"You never told me that this CD was for Naomi. You said you were just working out to it. You gave me only like eight songs to burn on there. How could I not fill in the *Superman* theme? I'm taking one song from the end of The Best of John Williams CD and I figured, how could he not want that theme if he's pumping up?"

"I don't know what she's talking about when she says Nazis," I say, afraid of that word. I run through what I wrote down for Travis to burn. I knew my music taste didn't match hers, and maybe sometimes I do think about the *Superman* theme when I think about her, so it might still work out as cute if she doesn't think I'm a Nazi.

"Did you put 'The Imperial March' on there because there's some pretty obvious correlations between the Empire and the Third Reich."

"Bigham, you're thinking all wrong. Nothing that you could possibly have put on there matters," Travis says.

"*You* put those songs on there. You did," I say, putting the ball under my left arm and pointing at him like my dad points at me. "I mean, I'm in love with the girl but not the kind where I hear 'Duel of the Fates' blare out around her when she walks in the room. You're telling me that that one's on there too?"

"Kyle said that the entire class laughed," says Travis. "For like ten minutes. Even the teacher who comes down from the community college laughed. Naomi laughed. Kyle laughed. Then one of her stuck-up girlfriends who Naomi sometimes sits with asked if she was talking about the fat kid who carries around that big black Five Star notebook."

"That notebook has poems about Naomi in it!" I say, kind of pacing, the ball in a light headlock.

"Bigham, if there was a trial to determine whether you were a virgin or not, that notebook would be people's Exhibit A," says Travis. "I'm saying this is majorly embarrassing, Bigham. And they think I had something to do with it too."

"You did! You put those songs in there! You made me look like a total dork!" I see Julie in the gym entryway, one hand on her hip, annoyed and waving me over. I'm just glad that she's somebody who's not Naomi, and I start to walk toward her and home and a five-hour nap.

"Dude, just tell everybody that it was totally all you, that I didn't have anything to do with it," says Travis.

"You are officially on the list of people who need to shut the fuck up right now," I yell back at him. Julie's already in the car when I walk out to the lot. As her car bumps down our driveway, I look down and see that I'm still holding the school's basketball in my hands.

When I wake up from the nap that kept me from killing myself, it's dark and my parents are asleep. I walk downstairs to get the phone to take it back up to my room. By the computer I have to look through the school's student/ teacher directory again to find Naomi's number, and that makes me even madder and more embarrassed because I will have only made two phone calls to Naomi's house, one to tell her that I love her and one to tell her that I hate her.

Maybe Naomi was just a little overwhelmed, though. Maybe during this phone call I can help to clear some things up. Step by step I can tell her that I'm not a Nazi, that I know the difference between being in love and being obsessed, and that there was some real affection behind the making of that CD.

I am a full two rings into calling her when I look at my alarm clock and find out that it's eleven o'clock at night and that my nap had gone on way too long, but before I can hang up Naomi's voice says, "Hello?" and the only thing worse than calling late and trying to explain yourself is calling late and hanging up and having your number on their caller ID.

"Hey, Naomi. This is Jacob," I say.

"Oh, gosh. Hey, Jacob. What's up? It's late," she says, yawning.

"I know that it's late, but I'm calling to clear things up about what you read in front of everybody in English today," I say. I can totally salvage this. I can turn this into something endearing. If I string together enough words in a logical order, then she won't think that I'm insane.

"Look, Jacob I just needed to get something off of my chest," says Naomi. "I'm sorry that you heard about it. Now you have my dad yelling at me for calling me so late," she says, her voice moving across the receiver so that I can tell she's turning her head to the side and making hapless explanatory gestures to her dad, like rolling her eyes as she loops an index finger over her left temple and mouths "That crazy guy."

"What's the point in keeping a journal if you're going to read it out loud in front of the entire class?" I ask.

"You don't have any right to be upset with me, frankly," she says. "I mean, you're the one calling me up out of nowhere, at all hours, like giving me this weird black CD and demanding that I listen to it," she says, parsing out her fake language. I mean, using words and phrases like "frankly" and "all hours." Like this is a deposition or something.

"I called twice, Naomi. Twice. Counting this one. I just don't understand why you're so freaked out by me," I say, wondering when she is going to stop saying stuff that upsets me so that I can concentrate on sounding nice and rational.

"Because you can't just start telling girls that you're in love with them. Duh. Then you want me to act like I'm in love with you, but I can't even act like I know you. We hang out at the same table, crack some jokes, that's it," she says.

"We worked the whole summer together!"

"Half a summer," she says. "Plus, I was a cashier and you were an usher. Those are like two different departments."

"Bullshit departments, like it was a Fortune 500 company or something. It was a theater. I can't understand how other guys get away with it. They also give mix CDs, and they call up. But I guarantee they don't feel as strongly about you as I do. I have no idea how I could feel a stronger feeling for you than I felt over the summer and up until today and maybe even after today. I know I'm not thin and my skin's not the best and that last year before I fell in love with you I had a bad bout of fat-kid farts at our table and kept letting them out because everyone there thought it was funny. Even you thought it was funny!" I say, pulling a random event from memory, one of the hundreds of social missteps I may have made that may have hobbled my chances with Naomi.

"Jacob. This conversation's getting messed up. You are getting angry and weird and acting all like you are entitled to me, but you're not," Naomi says, sounding like Mom trying to settle me down.

"I just don't see how this is possible," I say. "You humiliating me, you being scared of me. If you could just see how I felt…" My right jaw muscles have clenched so hard against the receiver that I've accidently put Naomi on hold.

"Wait, wait, Naomi, I didn't hang up," I say, reaching over for my notebook and opening it up to poems about Naomi:
"The stands of pine, their limbs entwined
With fireflies between their upper boughs
Like cracked Wintergreen Lifesavers
Before a windblown dip to kiss…"

"Jacob, are you reading this off from something?" Naomi asks, her voice growing higher. "Oh, Mr. Can't-Be-Written-About is reading off stuff he wrote about me. You are beyond creeping me out right now—at school, in the parking lot, everywhere. I can't even sit at our table anymore without Kyle or Travis teasing me that you're off making a sculpture of me in the middle of the football field. If you don't leave me alone, I will go to the cops or tell the headmaster or get something that warns you not to get near me, not to talk to me, to let me alone until I finally graduate and get out of this state, I swear."

"Naomi, c'mon. I'm not dangerous. This is just messed up all around," I say.

"Young man, this conversation is over," says a deep dad voice. "Don't call this house again. And tomorrow your guidance counselor's going to hear about what you've been putting Naomi through." And Naomi's dad hangs up.

CHAPTER 6

Three girls sit in front of me in trigonometry, and I can't stand the sound of the middle one's voice, Sarah, as she asks Mr. Welker to go over last night's homework one last time. It's not like she's technically dumb. She and her two friends do make slightly better grades than I do in this class, but it's just that one time Mr. Welker asked them who the vice president was and they didn't know, they just didn't. I've already done tonight's homework and am trying to read now, but these three girls are so dumb and sexy that I cannot concentrate.

In trig we don't have desks. We sit at those black, lacquered lab tables, and I have a table all to myself where I sit behind these girls and watch as they gossip before class, wearing these super-tight jeans and scooting up to sit on the front edge of the table to swing their pink sneakered feet until Mr. Welker barrels in. I've got to grit my teeth against the way the denim dents against the edge of the table.

When they finally sit down and lean forward, the backs of their sweaters jump upward and expose crescents of smooth backfat just barely beginning to accumulate over recent years since they stopped taking ballet and started sipping diet soda. I stayed up all last night, so I'm constantly nodding, about to fall asleep, so anyone sitting behind me sees three moons, pastel panties acting as the reflected light from the dingy blond sun of my setting head. Is there no higher pedigree of flesh than the backfat of high school girls? In the fall it's the only spot of them exposed between the times they cheer at pep rallies, and in between the shutter blinks of my eyelids, I'm taking pictures so that I'll have something to reference today when I get home and beat off to anybody but Naomi. I want to rest my left cheek on that backfat and slowly write my name with the highlighters they bring in for math, a different color for every letter, fussily choosing each pen like an accomplished artist, hearing them inhale in anticipation as I pop the cap off each pen and also dip it in a neon inkwell for some reason. God, who brings highlighters for math?

"Jacob, are you paying attention?" asks Mr. Welker.

"Oh God, I feel awful Naomi—I mean, Mr. Welker."

"What?" He asks.

"Yeah, I mean I know this stuff," I say.

"I wasn't asking if you know it. I was asking if you were paying attention," he says, pushing his glasses up the bridge of his nose like a tamed ogre fitting a stone into a castle battlement.

And then a conspicuous absence of background sounds insulates my head. The thicker air, uncut by pen scratching and shuffling and whispering, keeps the heat inside my ears so that they turn red and seem to crisp from the inside out. Why is he coming down on me? Just give me one day, one day after getting my heart broken where I can nap like the rest of these idiots.

"I shouldn't have to pay attention if I already know the material," I say.

"Jacob, that is the exact opposite way you should be handling this situation right now," says Mr. Welker, clicking his pen really fast.

"I pay attention every day, every year," I argue back. "It shouldn't be paying attention. It should be saving attention, and from now until I graduate I'm going to just sit here and live off the interest."

"The fact that I've never had to yell at you before is the only thing keeping me from kicking you out right now. Now shut up, pay attention, and let's resume," he says.

"You should just leave me alone," I say.

Mr. Welker quickens his pen clicking. He is a big guy who used to play football for Notre Dame before he went into the air force, and I always thought that it'd be neat to have him for a dad. I liked him even before I had him as a teacher because every October during the school's harvest festival, the chaste Christian sister to public school

Halloween parties, Mr. Welker would pull almost every kid, including me, around the gym floor on a homemade hovercraft. And even though I weighed twice as much as any other kid, he never balked or acted like his back was hurting or called me "big fella" as I filled up the entire plywood circle and felt the leaf blowers void their warranties trying to lift me off the ground. Last year some football players helped him swing the kids in shifts, but the boys would always wait for either Mr. Welker or James to pull because that was when the hovercraft moved fastest. It had been Mr. Welker who had always joked about dying of a heart attack on the gym floor.

"I should leave you alone?" asks Mr. Welker. I can't look him in the eyes, so instead I concentrate on the furrows of forearm muscle that shift between each click. I think about someday gaining that kind of strength and sitting next to Mr. Welker on the bench in front of a black baby grand piano and laying our forearms down on the keys and playing "Chopsticks" together by twiddling our fingers and letting our muscles depress the keys like they did in *Big*, only with a real piano and with our forearms. I think of buying him the DVD of *Big* and giving it to him along with a note that apologizes for me going apeshit in his class like this.

"Whoa," I say. "Not like when you tell your parents to leave you alone or anything. I mean, like in the context of education, if I already know what you're trying to teach... If

I know what's going on, then you're just wasting your time with me, but wasting it in a good way."

"Jacob, are you all right? I mean, are you not feeling well?" asks Mr. Welker.

"What I said about you wasting your time came out all wrong. As a logical man with his own thoughts to think, you know what it's like—people staring at you and wasting your time like this," I say, in lieu of an apology, in lieu of just shutting up. "You know what? I think I'll just get out of here," I say to myself and get up and walk out the class-room door.

I don't run down the hall but power walk like my wife's already on her third lap around the mall and I'm just trying to keep pace. I turn the corner toward the computer lab where I know that Julie's in class. I open the door and peer in to find where she's sitting. Mr. Jefferson is out as usual, so everybody turns around when I open the door because they think I'm him.

"Julie, you need to give me the keys to the car. I have to go."

"What?" asks Julie. Naomi and Kyle are in the corner of the class opposite to Julie, sitting by each other. Their chairs are under the light panel that's always flickering on and off.

"I gotta drive away. It's an emergency dentist appoint-ment," motioning for her to throw me the keys.

"How can you have an emergency appointment?" Kyle asks and Naomi must not be too traumatized because I can hear her laugh.

"Mom said she will pick you up right after school, but this is serious. I need the keys," I say, with my arm still out-stretched. "Give me the keys."

I've been embarrassed to the point of numbness today, so even If I dropped to the carpet in pain and shuddered out a litter of kittens from my own ass, mewling through a slick coating of ass-afterbirth as they wobble blindly across the room toward Naomi, I'd still be able to get up with the runt dangling from under the cuff of my khakis and demand those keys.

"Keys," I say, still holding out my hand, knowing that Julie's stunned mind will latch onto the only word that can get her brother away from her.

"OK, here they are," she says, reaching down to unclip them from her backpack while still looking at me, like I've yelled at her to drop the gun. She tosses the keys toward me, the gesture also serving to shoo me out the door, and that's why the throw's so weak and the keys end up landing in the middle of the room. I walk to the middle of the room and can't help but glance over toward Naomi, and with that light flickering on and off, it looks like I was mistaken. Naomi and Kyle were not sitting by each other. Naomi was sitting in Kyle's lap.

When I walk out of the classroom, Mr. Welker is in the hallway waiting for me. His eyes look concerned behind his thick glasses, but it's the same concern you would show toward the raccoon hissing under your porch as you wonder whether to beat it out with a broom or call Animal Control.

"Jacob, you can't just leave like this," he says, hands out like I'm going to juke past him.

"I'm sick of this and I have to go home," I say.

"Jacob, if you're not feeling well, you can go to the school nurse. Otherwise, you're just being disruptive and I will send you to the guidance counselor."

"We don't have a school nurse. We just have a secretary with an ear thermometer and some Band-Aids," I say.

"This is completely unlike you, Jacob. I'm not used to ordering kids like you around. You had better control yourself if you want to come back to my class ever again," he says.

"I will never, ever, go back to that class and learn useless shit and get laughed at whenever I try to say something," I say.

"Jacob," he says, and this time it's not in the tone of a teacher running through the liability laws in their heads before they say something. It's the tone of a man pissed off at being defied. "You're done getting warnings."

Now I can't even look at him at all, just into the trophy case, which contains a plaque with his picture on it, the one and only year we won the state independent school baseball championship. He's staring me down on that plaque too.

"I thought you might have just been sick, but now I find out that you're just some little jerk trying to get away with whatever he can get away with," he says.

"No, Mr. Welker, it's not like that. If you just let me get away today, this will all be over," I say.

"You're going to the guidance counselor right now. You tell her what you told me, about my class being stupid shit. Then will see what she decides to do," he says. He takes me by the elbow and leads me down the hall, knocks on the Mrs. Bailey's door, and sticks his head in.

"I've got one for you," he says, as I lean against the whitewashed cinderblock wall a few feet behind me, wishing that the pitted pale brick would precisely interlock with the pitted pale skin of my acne-burst back, the wall turning round on hidden hinges, revealing a small safe room where there's a cot and a mini fridge full of roast beef sandwiches and bottles of Mountain Dew and a desk with a really fast computer on it where I don't have to dial out to the Internet.

"Who is it?" I can hear Mrs. Bailey ask from her desk.

"Jacob Bigham," says Mr. Welker.

"Is everything all right?" she asks with a hint of real fear in her voice.

"Not with him," says Mr. Welker, kind of smiling.

"Bob, I mean it," says Mrs. Bailey.

"No, he just refuses to listen in my class and got up to leave, and he needs to talk with you so we can figure out how to punish him," says Mr. Welker.

And he opens the door with a motion like dusting off his hands, and next I am sitting in front of the guidance counselor.

Why even try and describe the guidance counselor. I don't know. She's a woman between forty and fifty years old. She wears a lot of jewelry every day, and during Spirit Week when we have "Dress Like Your Favorite Teacher/Staff Member Day" a lot of girls choose her just so they have an excuse to raid the tops of their moms' dressers. In fact, this year there was an asterisk by her name on the fliers stapled up by the student council announcing that theme that said:

Due to parental complaints about lost or stolen jewelry, we ask that all students choosing to dress as Mrs. Bailey please either wear costume jewelry or make their own.

"So Jacob," says Mrs. Bailey, clinking a charm bracelet snake into the rim of the glass candy jar on the corner of her desk, offering one to me before taking one for herself. "What happened?"

"I just kind of stopped paying attention in his class and he wouldn't leave me alone about it," I say. "All I wanted was to go get the car keys from my sister and leave, and he chased me down the hallway."

"He chased you?" she asks.

"No, he didn't chase me. He was just standing there when I got out of Julie's class, but he looked like he was about to tackle me," I say.

Mrs. Bailey's office is a mess, and I almost kick over a pile of college pamphlets that are on a coffee table to my left while crossing my legs in the chair. Crossing my legs under my own power is still kind of a new thing for me because usually my thighs get in the way. Then a month ago I went through an awkward phase of being able to comfortably cross my legs but only after reaching down to grab the hem of my pants and pull up to lock my right leg in place. But now I can cross my legs completely under my own power, and I'm still just a little overenthusiastic about it, nearly scattering a hundred multiracial rainbows of smiling, well-adjusted individuals across her office carpet. Outside it's lunchtime for the elementary school, and I can hear them shouting in the courtyard below, high voices bouncing against the concrete, excited to eat.

"Jacob, I have to admit I'm not used to seeing you in trouble," Mrs. Bailey says, her hair hard silver and still closely cropped even years after the chemo.

"I know. I don't think I've ever been in trouble since fifth grade when I got here," I say, trying to keep eye contact with her, trying to let her know that I am here, with her, working things out. I think that today she's going to let me cash in on six years of keeping out of the way and get off with a warning.

"But frankly, it's just as well you're here now. We've received some complaints about your behavior from another student and I would have had to call you in here later today anyway," she says, leafing through some sheets of paper on her desk.

"What behavior?" I ask.

"Did you give a black CD to a certain student and then repeatedly call this student's house?" she asks. "Both this student and her father have told me about this issue."

"Mrs. Bailey, you don't have to say 'this student.' It's Naomi McKenzie and I've called her a total of two times, so I guess, yeah, that's a repetition, but it is not repeatedly," I say, but my heart speeds up under my coat, and I'm afraid that she'll see my buttons buzzing like raindrops on the hood of a rap star's car.

"Naomi told us that this black CD had some unsettling choices on it. Songs from violent video games? Songs having to do with Nazis?"

"Mrs. Bailey, there was nothing on that CD that had anything to do with Nazis. I don't know why people keep saying this. OK, now that I think about it, the CD has the theme from *Schindler's List* on it. Is that what she's talking about? It's a haunting violin solo. It's objectively good! That movie's anti-Nazi!"

"And why was it black?" she asks. The phone rings and she holds up a finger to stop me while she picks up the phone.

"Yes, well I'm discussing something with a student right now," she says, looking at me the entire time. "Mmm hmm. Yes. OK, well, I will call you back as soon as I get word."

"It was black because Travis had written on it thinking the CD was for something else, so I covered it up with marker. I didn't mean anything by it," I say.

"Now you're talking about Travis Gant, in your grade?" she asks.

"Yeah, Travis Gant. He's my friend," I say.

"And you and he planned this out together?" she asks, writing Travis's name on a notepad on her desk.

Jesus, OK, whatever.

"No, we didn't 'plan out' anything. I had trouble talking to Naomi, and I asked Travis to make a CD for me. And then I gave it to her and it didn't work out, so that's it," I say.

"Well, Jacob, we can't be too careful. Not after what's been happening in schools lately, and with your sudden weight loss, complaints from girls about you giving them disturbing music, you wearing all black with a trench coat..."

"It was *one* complaint from *one* girl. It's a pea coat, not a trench coat, and even if I wore a trench coat, I'm not going to shoot anybody," I say.

"Now, Jacob, I never said you were going to shoot anybody."

"You mentioned Columbine," I say. "I mean, those kids didn't get famous for selling the most World's Finest Chocolate."

"Is that all you think they are?" she asks, her eyes wide and magnified and blinking behind her glasses. "Famous? Because those young men did a monstrous thing. They stole innocent lives, and they shattered an entire community.

"No. No, my point is I'm not going to shoot myself or anyone else, and I'm not stalking Naomi. That is over and done with. I just, you know, had a crush on her, and she obviously wasn't that freaked out when she made fun of my CD *in her English class*. And it's not like I could call Naomi a third time to apologize, or else she'd really call the police." And this is the longest time I've ever had to explain myself to an adult ever, and it is exhausting, especially since I'm on trial for mowing down a row of classmates with a gun I don't even own. And if I was going to take somebody out, it'd be one person, and it'd be Connor. Except, I'm not ever going to do that because that would make me look like the bad guy and him look like the hero, and all I have to do is wait three years for him to crash his Jet Ski into a dock on Lake Murray and take two of his frat brothers with him.

"Do you get mad at your teachers and classmates? Do you feel angry?" she asks.

Well, now I do. God, why am I even listening to you, Mrs. Bailey? You're not a man who can beat me up, and you're not a woman who I want to fuck, so that puts you squarely in the category of who gives a good goddamn.

"Bottom line is that you don't understand crushes because no one's ever had one on you, and I don't need a school that I went to Quiz Bowl for turning around and suspecting me of being a potential mass murderer. The only thing I wanted was to not be bored today because I paid attention yesterday. If I was going to snap against guys who called me fat or girls who wouldn't give me the time of day, I would have done it the day after I got here." And with that I kick open my crossed legs, stand up, walk out the door, go to the parking lot, and drive home.

Later, haters.

CHAPTER 7

On the way down to the Sanders' pond, I press my stomach against their chain link fence, watching my gut bubble up between the rust-flecked diamonds of wire. I've never been able to whistle, but I rattle the fence a couple times and shout "Hey!" across his yard in the hopes that his Great Danes will lope down from their kennels behind the house and bite and tear and so disfigure my stomach that the doctor will be forced to give me a gastric bypass while stitching me up. Those dogs used to be so vicious that before he fed them Mr. Sanders had to place five separate metal dishes equidistant from each other around the base of a big rose bush so that the first dog that got to his dish was protectively hemmed from the others by thick thorns until he finished, causing the other dogs to have to run around and find their food and stand separately while they ate. But after four years of Mr. Sanders being nice to them, they've gone soft, and now their leader King yawns into the day's last shaft of sunlight before lying down to sneeze dust upon the backs of one of his brothers sleeping beside him, and I cannot believe they won't take time out of their day to gallop down and eat me. I pull my shirt down and walk the rest of the way toward the pond.

It's been a dry spring and a dry summer and from what Dad's said a dry fall, and I guess he's right because I can't remember the last time it rained, and the pond is almost half its usual size. Brown grass rings the outside of the pond, intermittently smoothed down today by the licked-in wind of an overbearing sky. On the far side of the pond, a willow tree is pressed toward the dirty water's edge by gangly pines who think it's fucking hilarious. I'm halfway through my first lap when I notice a raccoon's carcass floating with a languid counter-clockwise spin facedown about ten feet out from shore. Its limbs and tail are stretched out, and it's turning with the stately slowness of a gray and bloated snowflake, dark green scum collecting between its fingertips.

There hasn't been a more convenient time just not to show up to school for a couple of months than now. Now, after pissing off Mrs. Bailey, I won't even have the faculty on my side. They'll know everything about Jacob Bigham that students knew innately—that I can't talk to girls and that I do get freaked out and upset over stuff that other guys just shrug off or makes jokes about. They think I'm some sort of neo-Nazi stalker raised out in the wilderness, just another Internet kid waiting to go berserk. You know, if that's all Mr. Welker and Mrs. Bailey think of me after years of hard work, well, maybe I should bring a gun to school. It's not like

I'd shoot anyone; there's no one there that I respect enough to grace with punching them out in their prime.

OK, let's say I did go up to Dad's dresser and take his revolver loaded with six brass jacketed doses of fifteen-minute fame. Who would I shoot? Not Travis, I guess. I'd tell him beforehand, and nobody would believe him if he told. No girls. OK, I'd fire a couple rounds over the pretty table in the courtyard just for yelps, but I can't imagine outright hitting one of them. I'd definitely shoot Connor, especially if he tried to bull rush me or something I'd align the sight right at the cleft in his so dangerously unshaven chin.

Maybe, Kyle, especially if he says something smug, maybe something about not being able to wedge my fat forefinger into the trigger guard. It'll all lead back to my phone calls to Naomi, though, as the root of my rampage, and when the smoke literally clears, I'll have given her the greatest gift a girl could ever hope for: an uncomfortable subject she can turn her head away from if she hears people whisper my last name in class. It's the kind of drama every girl prays for, to suffer the loss of two great loves in high school, though the only thing that would stop me from killing Kyle is knowing that Travis would use it to get closer to Naomi. "Damn it, I know it's hard, Naomi," he'd say. "It's hard for all of us. They were my friends too."

I want to run, but the grass around the pond has been crisscrossed with undergrowth and blackberry vines. Even the two tire tracks from the bushhog are thick with plants knitting themselves together like a community trying to make sense of the terrible tragedy I'm about the unleash upon it. The vines make me high-step through a self-imposed agility drill that I can only keep up for about thirty seconds before I lapse back into my regular jogging pace.

On second thought, I'll probably just kill myself. Just get out of everybody's hair. I doubt they'll even make the janitor take the flag down to half-mast. And it would be so easy, just taking the shotgun down to the edge of the pond's sungrayed pier and letting my brains rain like bread crumbs across the water, my body collapsing back into the water where I'll float face down, me and the raccoon, our corpses crisscrossing the surface of the pond and sometimes touching, only to bounce off one another and float away again, an obscene screensaver that will keep the pond from burning its ugliness onto the monitor of God.

I've made it five laps and am squatting exhausted in the weeds in the dark when I hear Dad's truck rattling down the path to the pond. The truck comes to a stop in front of me, its headlights still on, and Dad climbs out and shouts for me to get in.

All the outside lights are on even at dusk when I follow Dad up the steps and into the house. Mom is sitting at the dining room table with her fingers to her temples like its tax time and looks up when Dad and I walk in. You'd think she'd have heard us walking on the porch, but she must have been concentrating or nodding off. She's still wearing the jacket for her pantsuit at work even though she got off like two hours ago. The computer isn't on, but Julie's book bag is on the floor, so I guess a friend dropped her off or the parents picked her up.

"Yeah, yeah, I found him down by the pond. Nothing happened," Dad says, walking past her and back to the tool room to put his flashlight on his official flashlight rack.

Mom gets up from her chair and walks toward where I am standing with one foot on the bottom step and both hands on the railing about to rocket myself to my room and out of awkwardness.

"Jacob, before you go upstairs we have to talk to you about school today," she says, her voice quavering now and her eyes moving back and forth across my face.

"Was he about to run upstairs?" asks Dad, turning out of the tool room. "Oh, no sir, you're not running up to play Nintendo or beg off tired," he says. They call any video games I play Nintendo.

I go over to the rocking chair in the middle of the living room, which is next to the coffee table, and while I wait for my parents to yell at me, I pick up one of Mom's catalogs and flip through it, looking for a black trench coat. If I'm to play a part for my peers, I might as well get in costume. Honey, excited by the silence, confused by the family spread about the house in unfamiliar positions, gets up from her dog bed and comes to the chair, and I put down the catalog and start petting her. She's the only member of the family I plan on looking in the eye tonight.

First Mom walks behind me and sits on the left section on the sofa, which faces toward the television. Dad walks past me and sits on the right section of the sofa, which faces me, thereby completing the high court, the Axis of Admonishment, this green, coffee-stained, overstuffed nut-cracker, with the end table serving as its fulcrum.

"Now," says Dad, his arms at his sides, palms curled under the seat cushions of the couch.

"Jeff, can you turn on the light?" asks Mom. It is getting late and I guess with all the rush of their manhunt they for-got to turn on anything downstairs. In the minutes I've been in the house, it's gone from dusk to total darkness outside.

Dad reaches up to twist the light switch on the end table lamp but is still so pissed off at me that the ceramic lamp wob-bles on its wooden base and nearly tips over and crashes to the floor, but Dad steadies the lamp with his hand. The fleeing pheasant painted on the lamp's ceramic base and the scream-ing eagle inked into the underside of Dad's forearm eye one another for a tense second, but the pheasant backs down.

"Now," says Dad, squinting at me, "what the hell were you thinking doing what you did at school today?"

"Hmm?" continues Dad, while I still pet Honey, the nervous sweat from my palms dampening the short fur on her face. "We had a call from your guidance counselor waiting for us on the phone when we got home saying you had insulted her and stormed out of her office and caused all kinds of trouble that we didn't raise you to cause. Hmm, son, hmm?" he stresses, the tone designed to provoke, but I can't look up.

"Julie was in tears when we got home," says Mom, about to cry, and with Dad about to yell and Mom about to cry, it's a lava locomotive about to hit a stalled school bus made of ice, and I'm the resulting steam wanting to escape upstairs. "Julie said that you came into the computer lab and caused a big scene and then left her there after you took her keys, but when we got home we couldn't find you, and we thought…" but she's crying now with her face all stretched out, and I can't look at her face when Mom cries, only at the gray above her ears, which she forgets when she dyes her hair.

"I'm sorry I left Julie at school, but I was so tired of getting talked down to and yelled at, and now I have to listen to it here too?" I ask. Honey has passed from my hands and trots over to Dad, who snaps his fingers at her and says to get. Honey braves the passage between the coffee table and Dad's legs bolted firmly to the floor and heads over to Mom, who pets her absentmindedly.

"Yeah, you're going to hear it here. And you're not going to insult us and storm out, are you?" asks Dad.

"Are you?" asks Dad.

"No, I'm not. And Mrs. Bailey insulted me first. She accused me of planning on killing people! How am I supposed to respond when someone, you know, levels that kind of accusation at me?" I say, reaching back into the vocabulary of my courtroom drama unconscious to help me deal with this controversy I'm not used to.

"Bullshit, bullshit, *bullshit*," says Dad. "Mrs. Bailey brought you in because she was worried about you, and from what she told us and how you're acting now, I think she had a point," he says.

"Now, what is all this we hear about how you keep calling a girl at school and that you've given her a black CD with all sorts of weird music?" he asks.

"I'm not stalking her, and there wasn't anything about Nazis on that CD; that was all Mrs. Bailey making stuff up." I say.

"Honey, we didn't hear anything like that. We just heard that you kept calling this girl and that she was a little scared of you," Mom says.

"Oh. Well, Mrs. Bailey accused me of all that too, but I called this girl twice. So that's not stalking, I don't think, and I don't know why she got so freaked out. I didn't threaten her. And the CD was black and had all that weird music on it because I gave it to Travis to burn and didn't tell him what it was for," I say.

"Burn?" asks Mom.

"To put the music on, Mom. And after Naomi told me to stop calling her, I stopped. I try not to even look at her anymore," I say.

"So Naomi's her name?" Mom asks, but hearing Mom say Naomi's name is pretty terrible for me. "Jacob, do you have a crush on this girl? Is that why you've been acting so strangely at school?"

"Answer your Mom. She's being nicer to you than I will," says Dad.

"Yes, but I don't have a crush on her anymore. I really did think I was in love with her, though. And I was never going to hurt anybody. When they said that, it just got me angry, to know that they think I would do that. I'm not a psycho like those kids were. I just wanted to talk to her," I say. I never thought about hurting anybody until they accused me of planning to.

"Jacob," says Mom. "Jacob, everybody understands how that feels. But you don't need to act how you're acting about it, yelling back at your teachers, making me tear my hair out worrying where you've been. And you can't make girls feel back to you what you feel for them out of nowhere. Besides, Naomi and Mrs. Bailey and all your teachers down at Stonewall… I'm sure they don't think you're really like that.

It's just them reacting too, I guess," she pauses, and gets the look on her face when she's trying to open one of those round clasps on her necklaces with her thumbnail, "it's not 'stalking' or hate. It's just a...a misinterpreted intensity."

"Oh, thanks so much, English-major Mom," I say. And *she knows* I get maddest when people try and tell me why I'm acting like I'm acting or why I'm feeling like I'm feeling.

Before I can react, Dad's balling the front of my T-shirt in his fist and twisting like he's trying to squeeze out the sweat, pushing me back against the chair's runners, and I kick out involuntarily to balance myself but accidentally hit his knee, and for a moment I'm afraid he thinks I'm fighting him instead of trying not to tip over.

"I told you that you weren't going to talk to us like that, now didn't I? Now you're not. Are you talking to us like that?" he yells, only I can't think of him yelling at me all at once. His throat is yelling at me, and the air from his throat is yelling across my face.

"Jeff, stop it! Stop!" says Mom, stretching her arms out toward us in shock, not even thinking of getting up.

"I didn't do anything weird! I didn't do anything!" I say. "They're the ones giving me a hard time. I'm not going to hurt anybody. You know me, I'm not messed up! I'm sorry, Mom, I didn't mean to say that to you," I say. "Quit it, Dad! C'mon, please!"

Dad lets go of my shirt and I rock forward fast after he takes a step back, so both my feet slam against the floor. Dad stands over me and points his finger at me, his eyes shaded by the brim of his hat and the darkness of the house and the deep voice that accesses a hundred redundant sub-routines of shame. I haven't seen him this mad since the time I destroyed the microwave while trying to heat a mug filled with dishwashing soap for forty-five minutes in the hopes of rapidly cleaning the Warhammer figurines lying inside of it.

"I don't know why you felt like you had to cause such a fuss, and leave your sister, and tell off your teachers, and scare one of Julie's friends half to death, and have people thinking that you're going to kill people and maybe kill yourself!"

"Dad, I can explain this. This is all wrong." I say.

"What did I want to hear first from you?" Dad asks, still standing over me. "I'm not going to be one of those dads who didn't do anything while their son went nuts."

"I'm not going to hurt anybody," I say, "And I'm not going to kill myself."

CHAPTER 8

The next morning I wake up early and put on the closest thing to dress clothes I have left, my black polyester blend theater pants and the one white theater shirt that has the barest beginning of armpit plaque. I also manage to eat breakfast on the weekend, the first time I have done so since the morning I drove to take the PSAT.

While coming out of our driveway and down the red dirt road, I see deer hunters stationed in fifty-yard increments on the roadside. Some sit in lawn chairs with their guns across their laps or kneel beside electric transformers in blue jeans and camouflage baseball hats, racks of metal hound dog cages shining from the beds of their pickup trucks. So this is what happens when your school thinks you're going to flip out. They hire hunters to establish a perimeter around your house.

I have the good fortune to be hired by the first place that I apply to, a supermarket that's a fifteen-minute drive from my house. I think that working at a supermarket will be good for me even though I am trying to lose weight. Mom says that once you work in a restaurant's kitchen, you'll never want to eat there again. Maybe by working in a grocery store it'll help me associate my only one real pleasure in life with incredibly boring work, and I'll finally just become immune to food.

"I'm glad you applied," says the woman who I guess, after that phrase, will become my manager. She flips over the first page of the application I had filled out on the bench outside. "We were hurting for kids to apply. We had one leave for the air force and another one of our baggers, Edward—well, he's not a kid, he's in his forties—had to move."

We're sitting in the break room at the back of the store, in a table exactly like the ones in the cafeteria at school, which is a terrifying omen, but the job search has already gone this far, and I hate asking for applications and having people behind the counter giving me a disappointed look at the mere prospect of having to work with me.

The woman is black, but whatever, and luckily I came to this impromptu interview wearing exactly what they want me to wear if I'm hired. I sport the same servile dichotomy they required of me when I was working for minimum wage, black pants and a white shirt, though now that I'm about to make $5.40 an hour, I can indulge in the luxury of wearing a white polo shirt, and I no longer have to wear a bowtie. The woman has braids that come up in a bun at the back of her head and is very nice to me, laying her hand down on the cafeteria table every time she says "Now," between each point in the interview.

"Now, let's see. Don't you hate that test they give you? You know when they ask you if you're going to steal or not in like twenty-seven different ways," Keisha asks. "Well, let's see you answered no to all the stealing questions, so we're glad to have you here."

I start work tomorrow and go home to tell Mom and Dad that I have a job. When they go to bat for me in a conference with Mrs. Bailey, they cite this as a positive reaction to a very unfortunate misunderstanding, and I am not suspended and privileged to experience an even deeper level of shunning from my classmates as I head back to school.

I work from five to eleven o'clock most weeknights with LaShawn, the senior bagger here, and we don't talk much because it's not rocket science, which is what LaShawn says after everything he tells me how to do. The only time LaShawn has laughed at anything I've said was when I got a little too into the refrain of "Big Yellow Taxi" playing over the loudspeakers and he caught me singing along both in a really high pitch and under my breath. He's really quiet, so he didn't laugh out loud; he just rocked back so hard his sneakers squeaked and he clapped his hands together then shook his head. I was already jumpy because I was blocking merchandise, which means to pull stuff from the back of the shelves to the front to make the store seem a place of unending abundance. I equated it in my mind to stuffing the store's bra, of making the store seem to have more than it had. I had both hands around two-pound cans of diced peaches in heavy syrup, and I was thinking of a single slice sliding around the inner silver of a huge spoon and maybe about to get hard but I was also singing, so I was beyond embarrassed by LaShawn discovering me in that rare and sacred space.

Right after I come home from school I jog as many times as I can around the pond, hustle up the hill, and drive to work. At work I'm on my feet and moving the entire time, especially around ten thirty when we bring in all the carts from the parking lot. LaShawn brings in long lines of carts from the cart return while I round up strays from all around the lot, separating some as they try to mate with their rambunctious but stunted Dollar General cousins, lifting them by the scruff of their handles off the concrete-lipped islands where they've dined all day, across an asphalt pasture, and into the ass of the clattering dragon that LaShawn coaxes into the store.

I had almost forgotten Connor's laugh. When I hear it again, I am down on one knee cradling the capped but shattered skull of a jar of spaghetti sauce, the rest of the jar an oregano-flecked crime scene leak across the floor, and some of the splash is already dried to powder across the bottom shelf of the aisle that I'll probably have to chip off with a spare bonus card I found in the parking lot today. I think for a second that hearing Connor's laugh must be another sort of hallucination brought on by concentrating too hard on my new job, just like how for a second my mind was paralyzed by the thought of there being no spaghetti on the floor, because that's the thing you expect to see when you clean up spaghetti sauce. But as I try to pick the slim, flimsy of a mushroom slice off of a freshly waxed floor, I hear Connor's laugh again, and my manager Keisha's laugh, and the mushroom slice's laugh as it giggles between my rubber-gloved thumb and forefinger.

Connor is in the store. Now, I had prepared myself to see people from Stonewall shopping here. It's one of the big three grocery stores in town. I had steeled myself against seeing Mr. Welker or Angel Lopez, who's pretty much guaranteed homecoming queen even with that unsettling birthmark on her face that I either have to fantasize around or fetishize to an extreme, or even that dad who directs people where to park at soccer games, who has his own reflective vest and a piece of red-painted plastic taped around the end of his flashlight so he can wave SUVs around the track field tarmac. But not Connor, and certainly not Connor's laugh. I can't bear it. I will the mushroom sliver to sprout a single silver stud as it becomes Connor's ear so I can drag him out of the doors and across the parking lot by it. Now I hear Keisha calling my name over the loudspeaker, and I throw my gloves into the ringer on top of my mop bucket and come up front.

The tips of Keisha's fingers and her long painted nails are on Connor's shoulders, and she's still laughing while Connor imitates the sound of screeching tires and acts like he's turning the wheel of an imaginary car hand over hand. He is also acting like he's stomping on the brake, and I notice the two tendons on the top of his feet flex under his ankle socks that rim the tops of his new, white, unscuffed sneakers. Keisha finally gets a hold of herself as I walk up, and she tells Connor to "Quit it, Connor, just quit it."

"Hey, Jake, this is Connor," says Keisha. "He's going to be working as a new bagger starting today, so I'd like you to show him how we do things here."

"Hey, Jacob, good to meet you," says Connor, bringing his hand around for an exaggerated handshake, his elbow a perfect ninety degrees, his hand arcing up then down into mine as if in pantomime, like I'm a little kid and he's teaching me how to shake hands.

"I like to give the newest bagger to the next newest bagger, not only because Jake works hard and has the hang of it, but because he remembers what it's like to be new," says Keisha. "Not like LaShawn doesn't do a good job, though," she says loudly over my shoulder, and we all turn to LaShawn, who gives us a thumbs-up after putting another bag in a cart.

"Well," says Keisha, "Jake's in charge of your training. Just say around until closing, try to help out, and we'll work on that dress code tomorrow," she tells Connor.

Connor is wearing brown cargo shorts and what must be his best white polo shirt with a green stripe across the chest and I think some Oakleys clasped over the collar.

"Hey, Connor," I say. "Well, I mean, we are baggers and there's a customer so let's bag. That's like ninety percent of it." I think about motioning him to the conveyor belt at the end of the checkout counter, but instead I just walk over there.

"OK, Jacob," says Connor. "Dude, this must be an awesome job for you. Look at all this food. You must be stealing tons at night in your truck. Bad move, grocery store."

"Yes, Connor, I am fat and I work at a grocery store. This is a dream job," I say, waiting for the bright orange box of Tide to eddy against the smooth aluminum lip at the end of the conveyor.

"Jacob," says Connor, "how about I put this shit in bags and you can just do this," and Connor gets down on his knees and acts like the conveyor is guiding the food directly into his mouth, like it's an assembly line designed just to feed people like me, and he makes exaggerated chomping noises and loudly announces what item he's eating.

"Ooh chips," says Connor and chomps. "Ooh yogurt," says Connor and chomps. Cindy the cashier actually laughs, and the young mother still unloading her groceries from the cart turns around to see what's so funny. She turns so fast that her ponytail snaps around to cover her mouth, and I have to wait until the ponytail drops to decide if she looks dumb or not. She does. She laughs at Connor too. I smile and wait as Cindy hands Connor the "PAID" sticker that he puts on the pack of bottled water. Their finger-tips touch, and I can't wait until I find them making out in produce.

"So basically just don't overload them, and try for eight items in a bag. And like the frozen stuff is separate and the fragile stuff is separate. And keep the chemicals and cleaning materials together and that's it," I say. "And the rest is like mopping and that's it."

"OK, Jacob," says Connor. "Hey, why do you like being called 'Jake' here when everyone at Stonewall calls you Jacob? Does that name make you work harder? Is it like being a mountain man or a lumberjack or something?"

"No," I say, taking the shrink-wrapped box of bottled water off of the bottom rack of the cart where Connor put it and instead placing the water inside the cart itself so it doesn't slide onto the parking lot when the customer stops the cart. The customer thanks me and walks out. "No, it's because they didn't have any 'C' stickers when I got here so I had to switch to Jake."

"Really?" asks Connor. "They found some 'Cs' for me," he says, pointing to his nametag with both index fingers at once.

"That's no surprise. I mean, you kind of have a monopoly on them at school," I say, devastating him.

"Oh no, smart joke," says Connor.

"Yeah, well, you started it with the fat jokes," I say.

"That's OK," says Connor. "I'm only working here until my dad forgets about me crashing the car. You're just starting to get used to it for life."

"No I'm not. I'm going to college," I say.

"Bigham, everybody at Stonewall is going to college, but you're not going to have any fun there. You're just going to stay in your dorm room playing video games and not showering until your parents pick you up and you never go back. Don't worry, I'll remember you when I graduate. I'll let you have a trailer for cheap, and you can live right behind this store. I don't know what kind of trailer would fit you by then. I'll get you a double-wide. Maybe a triple-wide."

There aren't any customers checking out but there are some coming in, and I can't just stand there being hammered by Connor all afternoon. Keisha put me in charge and I'm going to set things straight. Now I actually motion him over to the cage of inflatable balls behind the wall of drastically discounted school supplies.

"All right, Connor, you're gonna need to leave me alone here if we're gonna get through a shift, because we barely see each other at school, but here we can't avoid it," I say. "Let's just not say anything to each other anymore, and you can goof around until you're fired."

"Pft...like this is an important job," says Connor, palming an orange ball in his right hand and slamming it into his left.

"It serves an important purpose," I say. "I mean, everybody eats."

"Unless you get there first," Connor says, devastating me. "Hey," says Connor, looking down at the face of his huge silver watch that rattles around his thin wrist, "we've been talking for over five minutes. Does that mean you've fallen in love with me? That you're gonna call and cry about me and say Nazi stuff about dead animals until I hand the phone to my dad?"

"Hey, Connor, for the short time you work here can you not mention her? I won't tell anybody that you're working here," I say, about to be choked up. I haven't thought about Naomi in at least two weeks.

"Man, who are you going to tell, that faggot Travis? Ha ha, I heard Naomi has a restraining order out against you," Connor says.

"No she doesn't," I say. "And what did I just ask? What did I just get finished asking you?"

"Easy, big fella," says Connor. "You don't think I can remember what just happened? You think just because you have what the third highest average behind the two girls who do nothing but memorize shit that you're the only one who knows what's going on?" He tosses the ball back into the bottom of the cage and points down to my chest. "*You're* the fat faggot stalker, *you* only know what a pussy feels like because *you* are one, and *you* need to get out my face."

I break away from Connor and walk down to aisle five, the cereal aisle, and lean my hands against the display where you can select what kind of coffee beans you want ground and poured into a paper bag, and I breathe, trying to calm down. I tend to emphasize the vanilla, inhaling deeply, and place a stray bean between my teeth and squeeze, staring at my own darkened reflection in the black plastic, and I think about which food product would be best to sneak up from behind and bash Connor's head in with. It'd have to be heavy, and packaged in glass, and I settle on the largest jar of Planters peanuts because the top is narrowed and I can grip it like a club. I could push Connor's corpse into the cardboard compactor in the back, but I'd have wait until I'm eighteen to be allowed to operate it, and Connor would never work here for that long. I eat a bean and hyperventilate into a paper bag.

I manage to avoid Connor for the entire night, which isn't hard because it's a slow night and Connor's already managed to make LaShawn like him better than he does me, and when I turn down an aisle, I see Connor doing an impression of the way I walk, and LaShawn is laughing and actually slapping his knees and getting ready to do the impression himself before he sees me and stops, which I guess is a sign of respect. I clock out and dash through the first sliding glass door just as Keisha as saying "See you tomorrow" to Connor, and I am out of the airlock and in my truck by the time Connor bums a cigarette from Cindy and they sit together on the bench by the rack of mums out front.

On the highway home I stop by Walmart and to look for a weight set. I can't find one in sporting goods at first and ask an associate where I can find a curling iron, and he points me back toward health and beauty before I say, embarrassed, "No, I'm sorry, I mean like this," and make a lame little motion that I'm lifting weights.

I buy a screw-together curling bar and a stack of ten-pound plates and two twenty-five-pound plates, making sure that the aisle is clear so nobody sees me weakly clearing the last two over top of the cart after a long day of hating at work. I also make sure to turn over the final plates of each type so that the barcode is showing and I won't have to lift the weights onto the conveyer belt. On the way to the checkout, unaccustomed to the momentum generated by a cart full of metal, I lose control and knock an entire line of scented candles off the shelf, but luckily they are just blocks of wax wrapped in plastic and not in glass bases, and they just thock to the floor. One candle lands in my cart, base down on a stack of weights, and I think about lighting it and letting red wax melt over the entirety of iron.

I pay for the weights with what remains of my second paycheck, and I carefully place them in the back of my truck. On the last paved road to my house I'm driving behind a maintenance guy's white van, paint-splattered ladders lashed to the top, and a deer jumps out in front of it. The van slams the brakes, and I see what was a deer buckle end over end onto the shoulder. Then I slam on my brakes, causing the weights to fly forward into the front of the bed of my truck. I can feel the impact in my lower back, and the shock causes my heart to skip. I decide that this is the deer's spirit, which has traveled through the van and settled into me and, and that night, while still channeling that animal energy, I lift weights on my back porch, lifting them over my head until gray fatigue paramecium float around the sides of my eyeballs.

I don't know how I can keep seeing Connor at school and then at work, but I know I won't quit before he does, because eventually his father will forgive him, or he'll quit and brag about it to me for a week, or he'll get a girlfriend so pretty that nobody will know why he ever took a job like this in the first place. I can still barely stand him though. Every time I see his name typed under mine on the work schedule I get a sick feeling of "about to be bullied." This is America, so I get the same feeling when I see a person's car as when I actually see that person, and I get nervous whenever Connor's car is circling the lot for the best space, even though I park as far away as possible for the sake of the customer. Oh yeah, he got a new car; it's a fucking Mustang that Connor says his uncle bought him just to piss off his dad.

My grandma has a picture of me standing outside of the Dixie Stampede when I was fourteen. In the picture I am wearing a black T-shirt that depicts an arctic fox prancing upon a field of snow that continues all the way to the hem of the shirt and down to my white sweatpants. There are pink stains around the front of these sweatpants, the faded remains of the fox's Kool-Aid kill that also dot the length of drawstring sinew trailing limply over my real penis inside. It's as if Connor has this picture airbrushed onto the hood of his car.

The next time that I'm forced to talk to Connor it's 11:00 p.m. and we are outside in the parking lot gathering carts. LaShawn is outside too because he's training to be a stocker, but he's on break now talking on his cell phone. He's sitting on the bench beside the white metal cage of propane tanks. We have already gotten all the carts that customers have wheeled to the stalls, and now we're rushing around trying to get the last carts that are scattered around the parking lot so we can clock out. It is finally starting to get cold outside, and I am wearing a black hooded sweatshirt over my work uniform.

There are carts all along the boundary between our parking lot and the Dollar General's parking lot, and the Dollar's General's smaller carts are sometimes shoved inside of ours, and it's a bitch to disentangle them. I am also picking up any trash I see on the islands that the parking lot sweeping machine cannot get—mostly soda cans—and putting the cans in the big front pocket of my sweatshirt. Normally I would put the cans in a stray plastic bag, but the only bag I see tonight is sticky with dried Mountain Dew and cedar chips from the garden center, fitfully billowing in the wind like the gasping gut of a morbidly obese hamster.

I wheel the Dollar General carts back in front of the Dollar General and am wheeling our carts back to our store when Connor starts to give me shit.

"Dude, you should wheel those little carts right in front of their door so they learn to clean up after themselves," says Connor, who is leaning on the handle of his line of carts and smoking a cigarette he bummed from LaShawn.

Connor, I'm not going to get in a cart war when it takes five seconds for me to wheel it over there," I say. I start to empty the soda cans from my jacket pocket and into the recycling bin.

"And don't put nasty cans into your pocket, dude, that's gross," says Connor, and he looks at LaShawn to see if he's laughing, but LaShawn is not.

"Connor, how about leaving me alone so I can clock out?" I say.

"All I'm saying is that if I looked like you, I wouldn't be adding any more junk to the front," says Connor, and now LaShawn is trying not to laugh, licking his lips as he flips open his cell phone to check the time. "Dude, you look pregnant," adds Connor.

"That's right, Connor, I'm pregnant with trash. Just like your mother was," I say, wanting to shut him up, wanting him to go berserk and kill me just so during his trial the court stenographer can crack up as she immortalizes my complete and total destruction of Connor's sanity with a single phrase.

LaShawn says, "Ohhhhh!" and starts to laugh and bends over double. I don't even want to look at Connor, I don't want to see his reaction because I'm so confident in the knowledge of my owning him right now, and if I see him get angry I might get intimidated. I walk through the first set of automatic doors and wait for them to close so I can depressurize when a cart rattles through and its lower guard bar crashes into my left Achilles tendon.

CHAPTER 9

Those automatic doors are pretty soundproof, so I doubt anybody inside the store heard me scream. That's the only positive thing that I can take away from this situation. Oh, that and the pain from the cart hitting me is so great that I don't feel that basket jam into my lower back before it spins out and crashes into the other line of carts. God it hurts, it really does. I think that this was how the Trojans finally killed Achilles, with an ornately carved shopping cart of fine Phoenician cedar, filled with jars of strong wine and wheels of fragrant cheeses. I hold tightly onto my ankle, reflexively at first, but also because my hands are still cold from outside. I look back through the clear doors and see that LaShawn is on the ground too, and a surge of adrenaline brings me to my feet, my foot, and I stand up because I think Connor has snapped and attacked LaShawn too. It turns out that LaShawn is rolling on the ground because he's laughing. He is laughing so hard at how I looked falling, my head snapping back, and I bet he heard a little of my scream. Connor is...doing something—jeez, I don't want to describe him. God, I hate his face.

To my credit I don't cry, even though the pain is so great that my vision is tinted red around the edges. I decide I can't walk back out through that door, so instead I grab the cart that hit me and lean on it like that one old Jiffy Lube guy who buys six Hungry-Man dinners and two gallons of pre-made sweet tea every Saturday. I use the cart as a crutch to hobble across the front of the store and right back out the second set of automatic doors. The first thing I do when I get into my truck is peel off my hooded sweatshirt because I'm panting from the exertion, and one more soda can rolls out of my sweatshirt and onto the floor. The floor is clean because the manager of the entire store parks his little Geo Tracker out here too, and I didn't want him to see my truck stuffed with trash. But now the cart I had to lean on to get out here is overturned right by the manager's space, and I'm in my truck trying not to cry like a totally chubby crippled slob. Connor is killing me. He is ruining my ruined life.

That same night I drive to Walmart again and park right next to a handicapped space and use one of their carts to help me walk around inside, though the pain has subsided a little. I buy a speed rope there because I know I won't be able to jog for at least a few days, and that night I try jumping rope in my front yard, just in range of the floodlights by the steaming compost heap. Even though I can only jump a few times on just one leg, my heart still beats faster than it ever has, and I breathe like a one-man Lamaze class, a man giving birth to himself. This is Friday night and I have work again at eight tomorrow morning.

I decide that my one goal at work is to outshine Connor in every respect and wait patiently for him to quit. I start arriving for work with a ten-minute lead time and bring a stray cart in from the parking lot every time I walk in. I pay attention to where every item is in the store, keeping an accurate inventory of every calorie that won't make its way inside me, so that when a customer asks me what aisle the Oreos are on I can tell them precisely where they are, and, if they're interested, precisely where they will never be. I'm talkin' bout mah mouth.

Whenever I mop I look for little bits of trash—twist ties and squashed grapes and super balls bounced once inside the store and lost and cried about across the parking lot. I shove these and the still-wet hairs torn from the head of my mop into my pockets and empty them all out into the trash in one go to save time.

Connor always stops when he mops to leaf through magazines or go up and bag for just one dude at Christina's aisle so he can talk to her for about three minutes. Or he just stands there and jokes about smoking pot and getting speeding tickets to the produce guy with the salt-and-pepper goatee. I see them still talking after I've already mopped my side of the store and the front. I shake my head in disapproval as I wheel my bucket through the butcher's area, and the warm water steams up from the bucket like Connor's breath as I'm straddling his chest and punching him down Mt. Everest.

Connor hates taking out the trash. And why shouldn't he? This was probably his only chore growing up and now, instead of it earning him new cars and nice clothes, he gets $5.40 an hour. He had one bag burst open on his non-regulation white and gray rugby shirt, and he flipped out and spent twenty minutes in the bathroom. He said he was not "a Mexican lady working at some hotel." I, however, know that by taking out the trash you are the midwife to society—that the people who clean are the ones who give permission for another day to take place.

The boss notices. The main boss of the entire store is Indian and with a long last name that people have a hard time pronouncing, so everybody calls him Mr. N. Mr. N noticed when I was limping after Connor pushed the cart into me and said that "he couldn't bear to have his best bagger hobbling about," and that comment just about healed me instantaneously. We even joked around one time when he walked through the back warehouse and asked me to stack up all the empty mini-pallets.

"I think we should call these mini-pallets, 'palettes'," I say.

"Yes, Jacob, I think we should. That would be funny," he says. "Also, can you stack those cases of broken salsa on the last palette?" he asks.

"You mean, you want me to make these cases of salsa more...palatable?" I ask.

Mr. N just repeats, "Yes I want you to stack all these cases on the last mini-pallet," and now he thinks that I'm dumb and not just continuing to try and make a joke.

Exercise is going well. I still go jogging as soon as I get home from school, and sometimes I take Honey with me. The months are cold and wet, and some days slivers of ice have frozen between the toes of the footprints Honey made the day before. My thighs are getting considerably thinner. They used to be inseparable but now are no longer close enough to chafe, and they don't scrape together when I jog or make a cupping sound when I sit down quickly. They are no longer speaking to each other. I can jog faster now, and I think of the air rushing faster between my thighs; I think of the air thinning like when it blows under a bridge or between tall buildings due to Bernoulli's Principle, but then *Bernoulli's Principle* sounds like a top-shelf pasta and I realize how hungry I am all of the time. That night after work I drink my first soda in three months, a toast to my irreconcilable thighs. It is delicious.

This is the same night where I have a terrifying nightmare about work, and I won't describe it to you because that's kind of a writer's no-no, but it is pretty scary nonetheless. Apparently I was shouting something in my sleep because my door creaks open and I can hear Mom's feet slide over the clean floor. I was just about to wake up on my own accord.

"Jacob?" says Mom as I turn over in my bed and turn on the light. "Jacob, are you awake?" she asks.

"I just turned on the light, so I have to be awake," I say, not disoriented enough to stop being sarcastic.

"Well, you were shouting in your sleep, sweetheart, so I'm just checking up on you," she says, and I search for her eyes, blinking, behind her glasses, which I never see her wear because she only wears them after she goes to bed to grade papers.

"No, I'm fine. I was just having a nightmare about work," I say, annoyed by the fact that there is another person in my room but trying not to be mean to my mom.

"Is everything all right at work and it's just that your mind's thinking about it?" asks Mom.

"Yeah, nothing's terrible there or anything. No shelves fell on me or anything. I'm OK," I say.

Mom has her hand on the frame of my doorway because she knows I don't like people other than me in my room, but she's still looking at me.

"That happens to everybody in this family. Your dad and I have both had dreams about work," she says. "Your dad had this dream that every box on his route had the heads of the people who lived there inside them," she says.

"Oh man, pretty scary," I say, hoping that this isn't the night where Mom tells me that Dad really is crazy but that together they've found strange strategies to combat it, and it's time that I find my own way of dealing with my inherited insanity.

"They weren't decapitated or bleeding. It was more just their plain heads. They were shouting at him about how he was such a bad mailman. He said had to stuff mail into their mouths to get them to be quiet," she says, miming shoving mail forward with both her hands and laughing. "He was really trying to do it with his hands in his sleep," she says.

I smile and shake my head, but I'm always worried about shouting something while I'm asleep. Specifically, I'm worried about shouting out Naomi's name because with exercise and work I've been nodding off a lot in class. Against my better judgment, I've also been fantasizing about Naomi a lot. I bought black briefs right before I really planned to start losing weight because I wanted the body of Bruce Lee or a Calvin Klein model and they only wear black underwear. They were too tight, and I had to stand up and rip apart the elastic around my legs, and I pretended that the sound of the elastic tearing was my shoulder muscles tearing out of my shirt as they flexed with the effort. Now that I've actually lost weight the underwear lies loose and blousy and rubs against my junk, rising and falling like breath with my alternately raging and flagging erections. Every day in my room when I change to go jogging I look down into my briefs at the shimmering snail trails of precum I've crissed across the insides of the black cotton, these pearl chip archipelagos, the outlines of my islands of desire. Star charts of the constellation *Desperation*.

Every time I see the beginnings of my seed all I think of is being dragged out of the classroom after shouting Naomi's name by two tight-lipped sheriff's deputies and having my underwear impounded, and I wonder how advanced they've gotten with DNA testing, whether they can determine exactly who I was fantasizing about just by the scrapings of my almost-ejaculate. I tell Mom all of this.

"Thanks for checking up on me, Mom," I say, actually comforted by her.

"Well, I know you've been running yourself ragged with the job and lifting weights and your normal school load," she says. "Your dad and I were worried that it might be too much for you, that you might be stressed out. You've lost so much weight, which is a good thing, but we don't want you to lose it under the wrong circumstances," she says.

"I want to lose weight under any circumstances," I say to myself, a few days later while jogging around the pond. It has been a long fall, and the leaves of one young sassafras tree have become so bright a yellow that it overwhelms my eyes when I rest my water bottle under it, so I rip off one of the few remaining leaves and smell it, trying to get another sense to help me bear so much color.

I can now do eight laps around the pond, which is just a little over two miles total and might wind the average senior citizen. I don't stop at all, though, which is a lot different than the first lap I tried, where every fifty yards my saliva tried to put out the fire in my chest. I supplement the last lap with ten sprints, back and forth across the straightest border of the pond, where I usually pretend that I am a Secret Service agent jogging around the grounds at Camp David and I hear that the president's just been shot, sometimes holding two fingers up to an imaginary earpiece to complete the fantasy, while Honey pretends to see a flock of wild turkeys, or a rabbit crossing our path, or she rushes to protect dog president Zeus, a harlequin Great Dane. Or she thinks nothing at all. She's a goddamn dog.

Today the torn remains of a popped pink balloon hang down from the branch of an oak tree over my jogging path, probably blown off of a street sign while marking the way to a girl's birthday party. The balloon is right at eye level—no it's lower, right at mouth level. I only notice it after it smacks me in the forehead, because while jogging past the oak, I have to look down and step higher over its exposed roots. Every lap after getting smacked I have to anticipate the balloon and jog to the right or left to avoid it, worried that I might look up at the last second and inhale it and fall to the ground choking on its shredded femininity. Honey, in lieu of performing the Heimlich maneuver, would bark then maybe sniff at my frothing face.

This balloon, something pink and pitiful dangling out from under an armful of Spanish moss, also reminds me of the time I gave a pep talk to my dick, holding my gut up with two hands and consoling, "Don't be upset. You are a great product. I've just failed to provide an appealing advertising platform to launch you from."

That balloon, which dangles so close to my mouth, also reminds me of the time when I was fourteen and tried to suck my own dick, lying back in my bed and trying to walk down the walls to my own awaiting face. My back had spasmed, causing my legs to kick up, and the toenails of my right foot had ripped my Wolverine poster. I keep the poster pinned up to this day because it totally looks like Wolverine is trying to claw out of the poster himself.

"Honey, that balloon is a foundering sailboat in a sea of shame," I say after sprints, sipping from my water bottle before making the jog back home. It is only right before I'm about to go to sleep, after work and a snack of baby carrots and peanut butter and weight lifting, that I think that I should have just reached up and ripped that balloon down, just ripped it down and tossed it into the woods, or into the pond, or into my pocket. And I think that whatever prevented me from thinking of just tearing that balloon down is an integral part of whatever's wrong with me.

The next day an old woman gets upset in the checkout line because she thinks she didn't get her second ham at half price.

"Don't worry, ma'am, we've been selling them all day," says Cindy. "You'll see that the price is less on your receipt."

"No, I was watching you ring it up," she says, "and when it beeped that sign gave the same price as the first ham," the woman says, pointing at the electronic sign by the card reader.

"Yes," says Cindy, "but after that there should have been a minus sign for half the price of the ham."

"I didn't catch that," says the woman, "and I'm not going to pay to see the receipt," she says.

"Well, I can just void it out and run it through again to see if it makes that minus sign," says Cindy. Cindy is actually nice to people, and I've long since forgiven her for flirting with Connor.

"OK, fine," says the woman, nodding at me, and I take the ham out of the bag and hand it to Cindy.

"Did it make that minus sign this time?" asks Cindy after running the ham through again.

"Yes, but now how will I know that I don't get charged for three hams? I don't know if I can see the receipt well enough to know if I've been cheated," she says. She still has a light blue hospital bracelet on, and when her lips tremble, she looks like Mom whenever she gets upset.

"Well," says Cindy, "I'm not trying to cheat you. I'm really not."

"Ma'am, I'll read the receipt with you just to make sure," I say. I don't possibly know how this could help.

The lady looks over at me for the first time and then down at my name tag that says "JAKE", a name you'd give a particularly dumb dog who lives to only please you, and she looks up at the hair I'd luckily combed for maybe the fifth time in my life and says, "OK, I can use another pair of eyes."

"Not that I don't trust you," she says to Cindy, and I know that if I had been handsome she wouldn't have let me help, because she would have thought Cindy and I were going to clock out with the hundreds of dollars we've stolen today and turn our bodies into a hot ham scamwich in a room at the Days Inn across the street. But the lady is still spry enough to remember a time when she would have found me totally unappealing sexually, and my ugliness lends me credibility.

Cindy rolls her eyes when she hands me the receipt, but I unroll it across the metal end of the checkout counter and start slowly tracing my finger down to where the hams are.

"I still can't see too clearly," says the lady, who smells like baby powder just like Naomi, and I hope to associate this smell with her wrinkled finger brushing against mine rather than scalloped yellow panty elastic stretched across the mole just above Naomi's butt crack. "I don't see well enough to know which items are the hams," she says.

"Well," I say, "these are the hams because they are two of the same items scanned one right after the other," I say, slowly circling them with my finger. "Plus, if you look over at the price, you can see how they're the most expensive items, which is why there's no wonder you're worried," I say, smiling up at her.

"Yes, exactly," she says, leaning closer toward the receipt.

"But the second one has a minus sign right after the price, unrelated to the next item on the receipt, and next to a number that is half the price of the hams, meaning it's half off," I say. The woman nods and I am still trying to think of how to prove to this woman, who is half-blind, that there are no more hams on the receipt.

"You see, if I trace my finger down the entire thing, there's no item on here that matches what you know looks like a ham being rung up, so that means you only got charged for one and that got you the other half off," I say, concluding my receipt-reading seminar.

"Well, all right, that sounds fine by me," she says, tightly rolling the receipt and placing it in her purse. She takes her money, all twenties, out of a bank envelope and hands them to Cindy, who makes a point to count back the change into the lady's hand.

"Ma'am, do you mind if I take this out for you?" I ask. "These hams, you know, they are heavy."

In the parking lot I bring the back hatch of her Windstar down very carefully, thinking how awful it would be to crush her neck or hands in the hatch after being so nice to her inside.

"I bet you think I'm one of those crazy old ladies who doesn't have any idea what's going on around them," she says.

"I did until you said that just now," I say. "But if you were that far gone you wouldn't even think to wonder how I think you look," I say, grabbing another abandoned cart nearby so I can wheel both it and hers inside.

"Exactly," she says. "You're exactly right, Jake," she says, trying out my name for the first time.

That night when I get home and toss my keys and wallet onto the dining room table, they land next to the box that contains my new jump rope, which Dad delivered today. The new rope is a thin steel cable with a plastic coating over it, and I thought that Dad would ask me about it, that he may be afraid that I was finally trying to find a rope strong enough to hang myself with. But beside the unopened box Dad has left his box cutter, which he carries around with him on the route to cut phonebook bindings or in case an old lady or a kid needs a package opened on their doorstep the very second it's delivered.

I have finally gotten comfortable enough with jumping rope not to scourge myself every five seconds. I'm actually pretty Rocky at it. Ten minutes into jumping and already the plastic has started to wear away from the middle of the rope. There is a square of bricks half-buried in the dirt in front of the stairs that lead up to our front porch, and now every time that the jump rope cable hits the bricks it creates a small spark, so I stop jumping and go inside to turn the porch lights out. While jumping I stare down at my feet starting to blur beneath the moonlight, averaging a spark for every ten spins, and I wonder how long it will take to jump myself thin—will I have to make a spark for every star in the night sky? How many briskly flicked bricks will it take to pave the way to my first kiss?

It's been a tough week for me. Naomi has officially started to date Kyle. During warmer days at lunch they sit alone on the brick border surrounding the Bradford pear planted in the courtyard. On colder days they stay in the computer lab. I've only heard this from Travis because I can't stand to see either of them. I am either in the library or in the back of the cafeteria eating a chicken patty without the bun and maybe some broccoli. In my most mature moments, I concede that Naomi is probably much happier with Kyle now than she could ever be with me. Kyle makes like fifteen bucks an hour doing IT work for his uncle on the weekends and has already been accepted by his college of choice, and he wears cologne and irons his pants and is generally not a maladjusted embarrassment like me. In fact, Kyle deserves a girl *prettier* than Naomi, a girl who doesn't pout her glittered lips and puff the spun sugar of her auburn bangs into the air in annoyance whenever Kyle gets really excited about programming languages. Often my most mature moments are reduced to endless fantasies about seeing Naomi publicly dumped and wailing under the Bradford pear. I have spent whole lunch hours praying for better men than me to break her heart.

The only time I've even taken the time to look at Naomi, besides sidelong glances at pep rallies, was when she left her purse at our nerd table before standing in the lunch line, and I got a look at her driver's license in the clear plastic pocket on the wallet propped out of the top of her purse to see how much she says she weighs. Even factoring in normal underestimation and some additional pounds she packed on since returning to "the States" (I've overheard her calling America "the States" like she didn't get her ears pierced at Claire's when she was eleven like every other girl here), I can definitely deadlift Naomi, though I cannot yet press her overhead.

So that is what I am trying to do tonight. I've wrapped an old towel around the center hump of the curling bar and covered that towel in a cocoon of Scotch tape so that the bar doesn't hurt me so much when I squat it. Over the last few months, the cocoon has caramelized when the inciden-tal dust of my hands and fingers mixes with the pressurized sweat streaming from my shoulders. I sweat so much that it soaks through my sweatshirt and into both tape and towel, making squishing noises as I slightly adjust the bar between squats, massaging my juices into the cocoon to feed the lar-val bar inside. A breeze is blowing in from the forest over the tips of my ears and the nape of my neck, and the bar is so light tonight that I come close to hallucinating wings spring-ing from the cocoon, and I press Naomi's weight once, then twice. After sitting down and sucking wind for what might be more than five minutes, I roll the curling bar away with my foot and stick my sneakers in a chink between a log in the wall and the porch to do sit-ups until I am completely wiped out. Despite being the most tired I've ever been, that night in the shower I still manage to clean and jerk it to Naomi.

My body's definitely getting stronger, but esthetically speaking, things have been going slowly. The edges, the outskirts of my body, are getting thinner, my fingers and feet. My calves are firmer, and my knee doesn't pockmark with overflow fat when I flex my leg out straight. I'm most proud of my forearms, now so sharply grooved that Naomi could slide her debit card across them and wait for the word "DENIED" to flash across my eyes, because she's got noth-ing, absolutely nothing, to offer me.

The once-sprawling suburbs of my gut have been demolished in favor of intensive urbanization, causing the hairs to be squashed further together in the mad rush upward to my belly button.

My face is thinner too, and when we went up to New Jersey to visit the cousins and grandparents for Christmas, everybody commented about how good I look. But I know that when they say that I look good they just mean that I look closer to normal, closer to a kid without something obviously wrong with him, and that's not what I want. I want to look *good*, I want to look strong, and the sooner I start looking legitimately good, the sooner I can start making up for the all the time where I was a sloppy and sullen waste of space.

The insects let me know that it is the middle of May. Gnats and mosquitoes start to appear around the pond, causing me to slap at my face and forehead at every other step, as if I'd just remembered something that needed to be done, and that something is to run another lap. I can run for much longer now, and I actually keep my head up and my back straight. The grass around the pond is high. Mr. Sanders mows it intermittently, but the weeds grow back too fast, and only the wheels on his tractor can actually kill them, leaving two small footpaths around the pond. Honey runs on the inside path around the pond and I run on the outside, and the leash threshes the weeds between us, while outstretched Bahia grass beats its seeds into my shins, causing more and coarser hair to grow there.

Every hour I spend outside has been in an effort to get more physically attractive, and so all through spring I've grown more sympathetic to Nature and its single, all-consuming struggle. The other afternoon while doing push-ups on the porch I saw a lizard, a brilliantly green anole, doing the same thing, pushing up in order to inflate his dewlap and have the afternoon sunshine stream though his erect red flesh, and it's the closest I've come to truly understanding an animal, only I've done the opposite and gotten rid of my double chin in my efforts to attract a mate.

"I totally understand you, dude, I totally do," I say to the lizard, and I think we synchronize for a bit, pushing up and down, breathing in and out.

I'm glad I'm good with lizards because otherwise this is the loneliest time of my life. Travis has had mono for the last couple months and got a new computer out of it. I bought the expansion to the latest game he was infatuated with and drove it over to his house, and he actually put down the mouse and introduced me to his parents before I shook his hand and told him I had to get to work. There's nobody at school who wants to talk to me, though I think that I'm no longer considered a deadly threat primed to explode at any time. I still qualify to be an honor marshall at Julie's graduation because they take the eight juniors with the highest averages from their entire high school career, not just this year, which is good because my grades have been relatively dismal, and I was not asked to participate in either the Quiz Bowl or the Geography Bee this year but who…gives…a…damn.

One day Kyle walks up to me at lunch and hands me an invitation to the big party he's throwing the Saturday after graduation. I notice that Naomi has not walked up with him.

"There's directions on my website, but you know the way there because of D and D," he says, handing me a glossy black business card with just the *Playboy* bunny symbol printed on the front, and on the back there's just a date, time, and his home page address. It's pretty fucking sweet.

"This is pretty fucking sweet Kyle," I say.

"Yeah, it's going to be one of those parties where people regret not being friends with you for the last four years," he says, and I only see him beam like that when Naomi removes the jacket she draped over the seat next to her to save him a place. No matter who he's going out with, though, I still like him. He's still a good guy.

"Kyle I have work that night, but if I can make it I promise I won't embarrass you or harass her," I say.

"Harass who?" asks Kyle.

"Your girlfriend," I say.

"Bigham," Kyle says, "Naomi knows you're not crazy, and I know that you wouldn't hurt anybody. That's why I'm inviting you. She feels sorry about how you were thought of afterward," he says. "So don't worry about it."

"Thanks," I say. "But what about Travis? Do you want me to take him another invitation?"

"I already e-mailed him," Kyle says.

Julie's so busy with graduation that we barely even see or speak to each other, but one time Dad made hot dogs and I said I couldn't run after eating hot dogs so could he save some in the fridge for me and Julie said, "Hot dog, more like not jog," and it's the first time I've actually laughed at something she said since we were really young kids. She also got a flat tire once right down the street from the grocery store and called me, and I went on break and walked down to help her change it, and that was nice.

Work is going OK. I now make $6.50 an hour, same as LaShawn but more than Connor. Connor and I continue to work through our issues. He was out all last week because he said his mom was in the hospital, which I don't buy and neither does LaShawn, and LaShawn rolled his eyes when he talked about Connor always having to leave work early, which means that LaShawn sees me as a peer and Connor as a liability. This is all irrelevant to Connor because he now has a girlfriend from North Carolina who is supposed to possess an almost mythic level of hotness—an unreal, unbelievable doability that just serves to reinforce North Carolina's reputation as "the better Carolina." Connor says that she's posed in fashion magazines before, but he won't bring them in to show people at school because, he says, "That's something you'd pull, Bigham. Bring a magazine in and point to a model and say that a beautiful woman was your girlfriend."

"She's coming down for Kyle's party, though," Connor says that Thursday, finally completing my collection of incentives not to attend, starting with *The Girl Who Accused You of Psychopathically Stalking Her is Dating the Host* and ending with a limited edition *The Guy Bullying You at Work is Going to Bring His Model Girlfriend*. This supposedly super-hot girlfriend is just the capstone to Connor's cool because when the yearbook came out, Connor had gotten himself in pictures with at least three clubs that he had nothing to do with, including, unbelievably, Homecoming Court, just by wearing a suit that day.

"Truly, this is the year of the Connor," I picture Connor saying to himself.

At graduation I am actually happy for Julie when I see her onstage, even though all the seniors are seated in alphabetical order and Kyle Marris and Naomi McKenzie are right beside each other in the row behind Julie. I am standing in the back of the auditorium as an usher, but when Julie gets up to get her diploma, I can still hear Mom sniffle as Dad winds the disposable camera.

I hold open one of the double doors for the graduating class as they exit the auditorium and out the front entrance of Stonewall so they can go throw their hats in the air. Julie makes a point to stop on the way out and kiss my cheek, but once the hats are in the air, Kyle and Naomi make a point to turn and kiss each other.

Mom and Dad walk out the door and to the side of the stream of parents, and Mom hugs me while I'm still holding the door handle and says, "Aww you're tearing up too."

Dad claps his hand on my shoulder and says, "Next year is your year, bud."

Naomi's dad walks past, and I overhear him saying, "I don't know where he is. I'm supposed to be on the lookout for some fat guy."

CHAPTER 10

That Saturday afternoon after I clock in for my five to eleven shift, LaShawn tells me that I just missed Connor.

"And his girlfriend was here. She bought him beer," says LaShawn.

"She's over twenty-one?" I ask.

"That's what the ID said," says a despondent Cindy.

"Was she as hot as Connor said she was?" I ask.

"Damn, man," says LaShawn, his eyes wide and his mouth half-open. And he makes the hourglass figure with his hand.

"It was more like this," says Cindy and pauses after making the boob part of the hourglass before making an even bigger butt part of the hourglass. "She was very pretty, though," she says, probably thinking back to all the times she's made out with Connor and how now he's doing it with someone so much prettier than her. "And she was nice, and that made Connor act much nicer. It was disgusting."

"And tall," says LaShawn, reaching his hand up as far as it can go, "She was a little taller than Connor."

Now I think that I might be able to stop by Kyle's party tonight. Travis had called me on my way to the grocery store and said that if I didn't show up to this party he would find a better friend for senior year, plus with Connor's out-of-town super-banging girlfriend there, he won't have the option to pick on me. He'll just spend the entire night trying to be as magnanimous as possible.

By the time I get to Kyle's, there are already cars lining both sides of the street in front of his house. Kyle's house is three stories tall and brick, its outside halogen lights ablaze. This house would be out in the middle of nowhere if there weren't other huge houses spaced about a hundred yards apart up and down his street that also want to be in the middle of nowhere. I park on the side of the street opposite of Kyle's house, the front right tire of my truck kicking up dust from the fallow peanut field. I stand for a minute by the side of my truck chewing gum.

The cars have been cleared from the top circle of concrete in front of Kyle's garage for a game of basketball. The players are all wearing baseball caps, brims bent almost double, and the glare of the houselights pools brightly on their polo'd shoulders as they miss shot after shot. Five out of eight of these seniors actually did play on Stonewall's basketball team, but our school is so small that we always hurt for able bodies, and this game shows why our record was so terrible. The only guy on our team who's good at basketball, a black six-foot-six exchange student from

Spain, is so cool that he decided to go to a bigger school's graduation party.

Just now the game has stopped because a no-look pass almost tore the driver's side mirror from Tad Simpson's Dodge Ram graduation present, and he is standing there beside his truck moving the mirror back and forth like he's rehabilitating a knee. Garrett and Cody Fulmer, our school's set of twins, are shouting at Tad to rejoin the game, and the sound of their shouts and the bounce of the ball on concrete pass through me and the mint gum in my mouth, through my truck, and across the peanut field, flying over the rows of recuperating earth to eventually collect in the red intermittence at the top of a radio tower, causing the light on top to blink on, then off. I spit my gum into a ditch and grab two cases of soda from the bed of my truck.

Kyle is throwing another set of keys in a bucket beside the beer pong table when I walk up to him, still holding the soda.

"Hey, Kyle, what's up?" I ask. "Do you want this inside or in the fridge?"

"Hey, Bigham, I'm glad you finally came," says Kyle, patting me on the shoulder. He is wearing a black suit and a red silk shirt, and he doesn't look like an emcee, he looks like a master of ceremonies. "Oh, thanks for the drinks. You can put them over there in the cooler by the beerbarrow," and he points to the side of his garage to a wheelbarrow full of ice and cans of beer.

"Jeez, Kyle, you went all out with this party," I say, impressed.

"Thanks," says Kyle. "I should have hired you to bounce. You are looking swole. Totally ripped. You always wear like a coat or sweatshirt at school."

"Yeah, thanks. I came over here right from work," I say.

"Here, I gotta take your keys even if you're not drinking," he says, motioning toward the bucket.

"Hold on, let me put these sodas away," and I go to the cooler, which is already full of beer, so I set the cases off to the side after grabbing a can for myself. This will be my second soda since I started dieting. I hand Kyle my keys.

"I'm only going to be here for a little while. Have you seen Travis?" I ask.

"He's inside, Bigham. Party hard," says Kyle.

The house is packed, but Travis is easy to spot. He's mixing drinks on the marble top of the island in Kyle's kitchen. I walk up to talk to him so I can cross the first of two items off my Kyle's party "To Do" list, the second item being to see Naomi for what might be the last time in my life.

"Hey, Travis, how are you feeling?" I ask as he pours liquor down a line of plastic cups that are a quarter filled with Coke.

"Feeling? I'm feeling great," says Travis. "Here, help me bring these drinks over to those girls on the couch," he says.

He brings three drinks in each hand, pinching over the sides of each cup so that liquor laps at his fingers. He offers the glasses around to the girls and they all say, "Thank you, Travis," except for the one in the center, Denise, who holds her hand up flat to prevent the drink from getting to her.

"Travis, did you just forget what I said?" she asks. Denise once went to Stonewall but left two years ago when she got pregnant.

"Oh shit, I forgot you were pregnant again," shouts Travis and all the girls beside her smile. Apparently Denise had picked this party to break the news that she is once again with child. Travis hands me the last drink to reach into his pocket and pull out his cell phone.

He flips the cell phone open and begins moving toward Denise, singing "Bye, bye Miss American pie, put my celly to your belly and the belly said Hi!" Travis pulls up Denise's shirt and holds his phone to that tiny spark of illegitimate life. "Hi there lil' belly!" And before she can react, he bends down and kisses her belly button, and Denise lets out a high-pitched giggle that is almost a scream and shoves Travis's head away with one hand while pulling down the front of her shirt with the other. Everybody laughs at how daring and charismatic Travis is. One girl even has liquor pouring from her nose and onto the loveseat.

"Travis, get away from me!" says Denise, still laughing.

"C'mon, Bigham, let's go outside," says Travis, leading me past four guys who are sitting on the floor playing
Goldeneye on Kyle's big screen TV and through the sliding
glass door to the party out back.

It is wall-to-wall people out on Kyle's deck. Some guys
from our football team are grilling steaks even though
it's close to midnight, and our starting tackle gets up to
check on his steak despite the fact that there's a super
drunk girl shouting on the trampoline and pulling up her
shirt at the apex of every jump. Travis and I stop to watch
for a while until her friends grab her by the wrists and
drag her down off the trampoline and she bangs her legs
against the top of a wooden box serving as a homemade
fireworks stand. The stand is almost black with the ashes
of what must have been a huge display. The girl is still
wailing loudly to be let go when she's dragged inside, her
streaming eyeliner accessorizing the ashes slashed across
her shins.

"This party is off the chain," I tell Travis as we walk off the
deck and onto the yard.

"I'm still searching for the chain that once held back this
mighty party," says Travis, lighting a cigar with a silver Zippo,
which explains the blue smoke I see everywhere. "I fear it
may be lost to us forever." Travis puffs on the cigar and then
stands there with it between his fore and middle fingers and

looks out on the party like a renegade colonel coolly survey-
ing an ongoing engagement.

"That was pretty cool what you did back there with
Denise," I say. "Everybody loved it. Did you think of that just
then, or do you still have a thing for Denise?" I ask.

"No, that's just a general strategy I thought up for pregnant girls at parties," says Travis, utterly serious.

"I had no idea she was pregnant again," I say.

"That bitch is forever pregnant," says Travis. "I'm just trying to get her friends to engage in the same behavior that's
getting Denise all this attention now. That's all Denise will
ever be remembered for—getting knocked up twice in high
school," says Travis.

"Dude, where'd you get that cigar?" I ask.

"Connor's giving them out. Dude, have you seen his girlfriend?" he asks.

"No, but I keep hearing how hot she is," I say, scanning
the yard for her.

"She is everything that Connor brags about, Bigham. I
would seriously kill Connor for her," he says.

"Please do it. Go ahead and live out my dream," I say,
also scanning for Connor.

"He still giving you a hard time at work?" asks Travis,
pulling a flask from his pocket and taking the half-empty
soda can out of my hand.

"Hey, whoa, I'm not drinking tonight," I say. "Plus, don't you still have mono?"

"Nope, totally cured," he says. "Least that's what I'm telling girls, tonight. Besides, this one is my personal flask," he says, pointing to his right pocket, hands around the other flask that he just poured into my soda can, and making me wonder how many brushed steel accessories he has on his person tonight.

"Bigham, you're like my best friend," says Travis. "I haven't seen you in weeks, I've never seen you drunk, and this party is awesome, and you're going to be a part of it," he says, handing me the flask, and I tip it toward my mouth and swallow.

"There's Connor's girlfriend in the gazebo," says Travis, who points to the opposite end of the yard.

And there, stretching both hands up to touch the Christmas light-twined arch in the entrance of the gazebo is the most transcendent example of human beauty ever to make the mistake of gracing this small South Carolina county with her presence. She is wearing a black-and-white-striped midriff that is so short as to almost be a bikini top, and when she stretches her entire midsection elongates to what must be three feet.

"Travis, check out her torso," I say, "It's like a torso, only more so." I look toward Travis, but he has already gone back inside to keep bothering Denise, probably to blow cigar smoke in her face in another cruel attempt to retard her baby just to get a reaction, and maybe he's already said something to me and I've ignored it, too busy staring at Connor's girlfriend's pierced belly button, a glittering lynch-pin holding every eye in place. God, her body is long. If a dwarf were to stick his tongue in her belly button and then lie flat and shuffle around in a circle like a human compass, his toes dusted in ochre, those ochre toes would barely tiger-stripe her lowest set of ribs. That dwarf would then get a high five from me, because that dwarf would be awesome. I guess high five for him, low five for me.

Connor's girlfriend turns around to walk back to the bench bordering the inside of the gazebo, and now I see that her breasts are just a gateway drug to her butt. She is wearing tight black pants and her butt is huge and ridiculous, totter-ing toward overripe. I hate it when guys cite how beautiful a girl is by giving measurements, but this girl's butt cannot be measured in inches; it should be measured in something that has a tinge of the Biblical, like cubits. Cubutts. Connor's girlfriend's butt is roughly one cubutt. And right there, still sipping liquor from my soda can, I have a long and involved standing fantasy about her butt.

It begins with me picking a fistful of lilacs in an open glen, and on the way back to my cabin, still shaking clods of rich sod from the impromptu bouquet's roots out onto the wavering prairie, Connor's girlfriend comes running out from the rough-hewn doorway, her calico skirts lifted in her hands so she can run faster. She grabs my hand and leads me into the cabin and undresses, and I begin to press the lilacs in between her buttocks to preserve inferior beauty betwixt the fat-filled covers of a two-word book. Those words? Alpha and Omega. I am concentrating so hard on that Butt in the flickering candlelight that I fall asleep on the Butt until it's morning and a mockingbird lands next to me and awakes me with song. But the mockingbird stops singing and begins to dig lilacs from the Butt with its beak, stuffing them in my nose until I sneeze, the snot turning into stars like Genie or Mufasa explaining something in a Disney movie, and all of a sudden Connor's girlfriend is shaking me awake in the sitting room of our Victorian mansion. Her dress is like a giant upturned scrap of lilac, only with a heart-shaped hole cut out in the back for her butt. We hunt for pheasant later that afternoon, and I deliberately miss because I know how killing distresses her.

Gosh, I'm glad I didn't work with her at the theater last summer and spend whole hours thinking about her because I might have actually gone on a rampage if Connor's girl-friend had denied me over the phone. In fact, obsessing over Naomi would have been step one of twelve in a program prescribed by Mrs. Bailey in order to wean me from fantasiz-ing about Connor's girlfriend. It's so unfair that Connor has her that it makes me upset. I want to try and steal her from him, I want to impress her and charm her, I want to call her Amazon dot bombshell and see if she laughs.

Connor's girlfriend finally sits down on the bench, shielding me from her butt and finally allowing me to try and find out who she's talking to. Apparently they are having a great discussion because Connor's girlfriend is really animated and laughing pretty hard. She has a big nose, but whatever. A gazebo post is blocking my view of the person sitting next to her, and I have to take a few steps to my left before I notice that this person has a black lace doily thing around her neck. It's Naomi. All this time she's been talking to Naomi. Seeing them together is the most upsetting image I've ever allowed into my mind. Now, more than anything, I need to pee.

On the way back through the house to Kyle's bathroom I see Nikki Chamberlain standing in the kitchen with an entire Twister mat wrapped plain side out around her, while Rachel Adams is kneeling down beside her tearing long strips of masking tape so that she can cinch the mat in the middle and make a dress. Two dudes who I've never seen before are at the sink. One guy has his bloody knee propped up on the counter and is trying to run it under the faucet, while his friend is holding a paper towel open under the refrigerator's ice maker, and they both keep shouting and laughing about wiping out in a go-cart on the peanut field. When Nikki staggers by the bloody-kneed dude at the sink, he reaches over to her chest and says, "Left hand yellow!" but Nikki calmly pushes his hand away and says, "No , this is my wedding dress," and when he tries again she says, "Noooooope," before walking toward the front door. The door is already open, and I see her gather the Twister skirt in her hands and bend down on Kyle's steps to pick a single pink tulip and place it in her hair before running to join the volleyball game on the front lawn.

Connor is walking out of the bathroom just as I walk up to it and we almost bump together in the darkened hall-way, where other rooms are playing three different songs as loudly as possible.

"Big HAM!" shouts Connor, shaking my hand while putting a new, unlit cigar in his mouth. "Bigham, Bigham, Bigham. My friend from the Food Lion! Hell, you are the food lion! Man this party is crazy!" says Connor, and he is in the best mood I've ever seen him in, his face red even in the dim light, sweat-plastered locks of blond hair leaking from under the rim of his backward Braves baseball cap. With his high-tops on and his bent-back laughing party aura, he looks about a foot taller than I'm used to seeing him.

"Hey, what's up, Connor," I say.

"Dude, this is a graduation party. Where's your sister?" he asks.

"She's on a date with her boyfriend. They are probably talking about getting engaged," I say.

"Dude, here," Connor says, fishing around in the pockets of his canvas skate shorts for a cigar. "I bet even you'd look cool smoking one of these," he says, handing me the cigar, which I wave away.

"I appreciate it, Connor, but I've been running a lot lately, and these would diminish my aerobic capacity," I say, sweating and almost slurring my words.

"Whatever, smart guy," says Connor. "Just take the cigar, man. Give it to somebody else. At our graduation party I'm gonna make you smoke one no matter how strong you get by then." And the fact that he is so jovial, so excited, and he talked about me getting stronger makes me actually like Connor for a second, and I take the cigar from him.

"Have you seen Angela?" he asks, and that must be his girlfriend's name, which is a relief to me because now in my mind I can refer to her by that name instead of always having to associate her with Connor.

"She's out back in the gazebo. I'll see you later. I really have to pee," I say, pointing toward the bathroom.

"Dude, are you drunk? Dude, you are! Bigham's drunk, Bigham's drunk!" I hear him shout as I close the bathroom door behind me.

In the toilet bowl is the stub of Connor's discarded cigar, and on the white tile floor there are Connor's footprints made from the mud in the backyard. There are footprints that show where he stood looking at the mirror straight on, then footprints from when he turned to the right and the left on that same tile, admiring himself from every possible angle before leaving the bathroom. While peeing I direct my stream to chase his cigar stub three whole laps around the bowl. It bobs and weaves like a hose-harried terrier before spinning into the middle of the bowl and I flush it down. I begin to take off my shirt before I walk in front of the mirror because I like to be surprised by my progress when I flex in front of other people's mirrors.

There's a big gray tick burrowed into my right shoulder. It must have hopped on me while I was jogging, and I focus on that tick while I flex my shoulders. It becomes the central point that my Magic Eye™ muscles pop out around. I've been concentrating on my shoulders more than any other muscle group, so much so that in the morning when I put my undershirt on backward I can tell because the front is stretched out.

I flex as hard as I possibly can, hoping at first that the tick will burst as the rich, red muscle blood rushes into it, but instead I begin to reach back for the tick, watching in the mirror as my waist narrows and my abdomen contracts. I pinch the tick off into the palm of my hand.

At first I want to drop the tick on the floor and squash it in the center of a tile right beside the one with Connor's muddy footprints. Maybe every guest at this party can claim a tile and mark it somehow as their own, the floor becoming an atlas showcasing the flags of every intoxicated nation that stumbled through the bathroom door. The bass from the party shakes the painting of the log cabin nailed to the wall above the toilet, and while still delicately pinching the kicking tick, I take the painting down to make sure that it doesn't fall in.

I study the tick and decide to spare it. This tick, like me, has grown too fat to defend itself, and it too deserves the chance to slim down and live. Then I think that being fat and crabby and weak-willed has always caused me to spend my time at parties noticing the stupidest shit. It's why the only people who benefit from me being at a party are lonely dogs and parents who hate throwing away food. At any social event I always frown and don't even try to be interesting or interested. I either latch onto Travis or look through the host's bookshelves. It's a big reason why I'll never have a girlfriend; because I personify insects more than I personify people.

I think that I'll quit this party while I'm ahead. I was legitimately invited and I contributed some drinks, had a laugh with Travis, and haven't embarrassed myself in front of Naomi. Plus, Connor remarked about how strong I am getting, and that might have been the greatest compliment I've gotten in my entire life. I open the bathroom window and flick the tick out into the bushes, then pull my shirt back over my head and begin to tuck it in, but at that point I begin to smile.

Usually, tucking in my shirt before a party or a job interview or a family reunion was a last-ditch effort to look neater and maybe fool some people into thinking that I might have my life together. When an obese person tries to cram in their shirt under a curtain of acned back and front fat, they usually make a first tight tuck, then they tease out the shirt so that it doesn't look like the stretched gray skin of a blood-drunk tick. A nervously tucked-in shirt leaves some pockets and billows of fabric under the gut, and when you walk out of the bathroom all sweaty, it's like you've spent the last five minutes hastily crimping the crust of the butterfly pie baking over your belt buckle.

Now when I tuck my shirt in my hand goes straight down the front of my pants and easily around my entire waistline, and I don't even have to do the post-tuck-in-fatboy-fluff-up that I had spent years perfecting. I'm still kind of fat, but I never thought I'd make it this far. I take some paper towels and wipe off Connor's muddy footprints from the floor. I fold my arms in front of my chest, using my hands to prop up my biceps, nod confidently to myself, and walk out the bathroom door to tell Travis and Kyle good-bye.

Someone has duct-taped a paper on the door across the hallway with "DO NOT DISTURB, BABYMAKIN' IN PROGRESS" written on it. This party is now totally out of control, and if I find either Travis or Kyle in the backyard, I'm going to say good-bye to one of them and leave as quickly as possible. I see Kyle and Naomi in the gazebo, sitting on the back bench and looking out over a game of tug-of-war in the backyard like a king and queen being entertained at court. Instead of a rope, the participants are using a tightly rolled Twister mat, and because the mat only holds three tuggers on each side, the rest of the teams hold on to the hips of the person in front of them. Nikki Chamberlain is second from the end on the right side, her wedding dress ripped from her to make the rope. She is wearing only her bra and panties, and she is laughing so hard that she almost falls and has to steady herself on the shoulder of the guy behind her. Hey, I think I went to Quiz Bowl with that guy.

I am waiting before trying to make it across the lawn because the game of tug-of-war is at its tensest and is about to fly apart when a girl's voice next to me asks if I'm about to join the army.

I had hoped that it was Angela, but the voice is coming from someone shorter than me, and when I turn to look at her, I recognize her as the editor of some other school's yearbook that I saw at Heather's party last summer. She's cut her black hair short, and I don't notice that she's lost weight so much as I notice that her boobs have gotten a little too big for her body.

"No, I'm not," I say, making an effort to smile at her. "Why do you ask?"

"Because you buzzed all your hair off, and you lost a lot of weight," she says. She sips from a straw coming out of Travis's flask.

"Well, so have you," I say, using the same tone of voice that Dad does when he meets a fellow banjo player and wants to convey his appreciation toward someone who's also struggled to make music under the hick stigma attached to the instrument.

She smiles and says, "I'm sorry I said 'a lot of weight' just now. I usually don't like it when people talk about how much weight I've lost even though they're just trying to be nice," she says looking away for a moment as the game of tug-of-war has kind of fallen apart but two football players are still pulling each other across the patio.

"I know. Whenever my family talks about how much weight I've lost now, I keep thinking of them holding back from talking about how overweight I was a year ago," I say, looking her in the eye, addressing her directly.

"Yes!" she says. "It's like complimenting me now is insulting me back in time," she says, totally getting it.

"Exactly," I say.

We are sitting in lawn chairs across from one another about ten feet away from the trampoline. We are both leaning forward, and her perfume seems to be everywhere, distracting me, causing me to dig one thumbnail under the other while I think of things to say to her.

"I'm glad I got to talk to you at this party," I say. "I heard you were smart."

"Who told you that?" she asks, nodding her head to the music she can hear from inside the house.

"The same guy who gave you that flask," I say.

"Oh, Travis," she says. "He used to go to my school before he transferred to yours. Here, do you want a sip?" she asks, offering me the flask.

"No thanks," I say. "I'm honestly just trying to wait until my buzz fades so I can drive out of here before the cops get called on us." My buzz?

"Oh yeah, I'm almost out of here too," she says. "This is crazy, I don't even go to your school. So Travis said I was smart?" she asks.

"Yeah. Usually when he has to admit that a girl is smart it's a pretty big deal to him," I say.

"We still talk sometimes. I was the first girl that he tried to kiss way back in seventh grade," she says.

"So you're her! You're the girl. He still talks about you sometimes, but he didn't mention that when we were at Heather's party," I say.

"Yeah, well, I think he was kind of ashamed of me at that party since I had blown up in the past couple years. I mean he'll go for anything, but he hadn't seen me in a while, and I think I surprised him," she says.

"I bet you surprised him tonight," I say.

"I did," she says. "He was shocked, and he gave me a hug, and he was really nice and apologetic, so I guess I don't hate him," she says, in the kind of singsong tone girls get when they talk about resolving a conflict.

"That's nice," I say. I guess I ignored her too at Heather's party, but it was more from shyness rather than the fact that she was fat. Lately I can find any girl in my age range attractive in at least one aspect. I watch weight-loss infomercials and imagine having three-ways with the before and after pictures. So here we are, stuck at Kyle's party, sexually reevaluating one another.

"I heard that you were smart too," she says. I know that Travis didn't tell her that, so I'm surprised someone else from Stonewall took the time to say something nice about me.

"I was but I took a year off," I say. "Now I just sleep at school and then go bag groceries."

"I'm not smart this year either. Didn't go to Math Meet, didn't edit the yearbook. I didn't want to take the pictures so much as I wanted to look normal in them," she says. "Is that part of how you lost weight, like at a job bagging groceries? It's kind of physical."

"Yeah, that helped. It keeps me moving all day, but it's also like the lowest job on earth. I lost about fifty pounds, but fifteen of those were my hopes and dreams," I say.

She laughs and looks down at my hands. "Plus, you have all those veins in your hands. I really like those," she says.

"Thanks, I'm trying to make them crawl all the way up my arms," I say, just as one of the football players gets choke-slammed onto the trampoline beside us. He rolls off and hits the ground laughing, kicking off a sandal at the guy who slammed him. They are not really fighting, but they are also not really paying attention to anybody around them, and Joanna and I have to jump out of the lawn chairs before we're bowled over.

"I gotta get out of here before they tear this house down," says Joanna.

"OK," I say. "But, wait, before you go, let me get your cell phone number or your IM name so I don't have to wait until I graduate to talk to you again," I say.

"OK, I'll give you both," she says and I write it down on a receipt for protein powder that I have in my wallet. I'm still at the stage where I'd hate to see my weight go up even if it is muscle, so I plan to return the unopened jar as soon as possible.

"OK, Jacob, it was nice talking to you," she says. "Come here and let me hug you."

And we hug and she squeezes me tighter, and I squeeze back harder than she can for half a second, my heart suddenly going so hard that I see her right breast reverberate beneath the beats. She notices too, and gasps, and I sort of act embarrassed and roll my eyes. She leans back and moves her pink fingernails over my triceps and rests them on the tops of my shoulders. My arms are incline planes, simple machines designed to make it easier for her to move her mouth to mine, until a glow-in-the-dark three-pronged foam boomerang-like device hits Joanna square in the side of her head. In her temple.

She drops Travis's flask and it hits right at the top of her foot, between the straps of her sandals, and some liquor splashes onto her sparkly toenails, probably peeling the polish right off.

"Oh, dude, girl I'm sorry! Oh shit, sorry about that!" and it's Connor. He is apologizing around a mouthful of his own forearm, the way drunk guys put their entire arm up to their mouth when they're really trying to express regret, and he has his other hand on Joanna's head, using his thumb to push back Joanna's hair to see if she's bleeding, which is almost certainly hurting her worse. He is shirtless and talking too loud and is super apologetic but only because Angela is also running up to examine Joanna, and Angela's breasts brush against my shoulder when she runs up behind me and stoops down to see if Joanna's all right.

"Honey, are you all right?" asks Angela, in a North Carolinian accent.

"Oh yeah, I'm fine," says Joanna. She puts her hand up to her temple to replace Connor's. "That thing just came out of nowhere. That's why I shouted." (Joanna had shouted, "Ow!")

"Do you want some ice or anything?" I ask, as the only genuinely concerned person. That three-pronged boomerang thing did just whiz out of nowhere, but it doesn't look like she's hurt that bad.

"No, Jacob, really. Thanks though, it was just foam." And I can tell she's kind of embarrassed because people are looking over at us, plus Connor and Angela are both much taller and better built than me and Joanna, so it looks like we're a developmentally disabled brother and sister who got scared by a seagull that snatched the soft pretzel we were sharing right out of our hands and our successful day-trader parents are running over to console us.

"Oh shit, it's the Big Ham!" shouts Connor, before Joanna can respond. Because it's dark maybe it took hearing my voice for him to recognize me, but it was probably just the visual disconnect of seeing me this close to a woman that took a sledgehammer to the bulbs in his tanning bed brain.

"Oh my gosh, Bigham. I'm sorry, dude," says Connor, starting to laugh. "I ruined your game. I totally broke your game," Connor says. "Be careful where you step everybody!" he shouts to everyone within earshot. "There's pieces of fat boy game all over the ground!"

"Connor!" says Angela, in model/actress shock, her hand still on Joanna's shoulder.

"Angela, this is Big Ham. This is the guy I work with at the grocery store," says Connor, jovially punching me on the shoulder as if he introduces everyone he knows with this level of disrespect.

"Oh good, well, you can start apologizing to him while I go with Joanna to get some ice, and you can stop apologizing when I get back," Angela says, leading Joanna away from the trampoline and toward Kyle's house. Joanna is still holding her head but turns to give me a little wave as she walks with Angela.

"Bigham, I really am sorry, dude," says Connor, scratching his left oblique apologetically, but he's still chuckling.

Instead of acknowledging his apology, I bend over to search for the cap to Travis's flask in the taller uncut grass near the legs of the trampoline.

"Bigham, did you hear me? I said I was sorry," says Connor, not laughing anymore. "You better answer me, Bigham."

"You know what? No, I'm not going to answer you because you're not sorry," I say, standing up. "You were laughing the whole time. You don't give a damn. You probably meant to hit her with that thing."

"Dude, I especially do give a damn considering the circumstances," says Connor. "That's probably the closest you've ever been to a girl, and I ruined it. And now you're going to go off crying and eating, and you'll go from regular fat back to being really fat again, and that'll be it for little Big Ham," he says, pointing down at my penis. "I'm just upset because you're going to blame it all on me."

"Connor, I'm tired of dealing with you, just go away," I say. "Smoke a joint, ride your Jet Ski, fuck your girlfriend on the hood of your Mustang, do all the things that make your life so much more awesome than mine, but your apology doesn't mean anything to me and you know it."

Connor steps square in front of me and puts his hands around my triceps and squeezes really hard. "Bigham, you must, you must be drunk to talk to me like that," says Connor, still squeezing, talking very slowly like he's lecturing to me or reasoning with me. And before I turn my body to wrench out of his grasp, I flex my triceps, and his eyes widen in surprise. Be careful, Connor. I can military press Naomi.

"Oh, man," says Connor. "You think you're smarter than me, and now you think you're stronger than me. I'm going to start cracking my knuckles, and by the time I get to my pinkie you better be on your knees, sucking my dick, accepting the hell out of my apology," he says. "One...two..." he says, cracking a knuckle with each number.

"Whoa, Connor, slow down. This is crazy," I say.

"I know it is, Bigham. I never thought I'd get this close to taking you down," he says.

"No, I mean the fact that you can count that far," I say. "It's going to take me a while to get over it." And before he can react I push him backward as hard as I can.

I think that hitting the small of your back against the ring of a trampoline is a pain on par with getting the under shelf of a shopping cart slammed into your Achilles tendon, and if Connor had stopped trying to fight me after that, I think I would have called things even between us. Connor is hurting so badly that he lies back onto the trampoline and starts rolling around, his hand on his back, his face contorting in pain as he shouts, "Goddamnit, Bigham!"

He's only on his back for a second before he gets up to walk around on the trampoline, still holding his back, mumbling to himself. When he comes back around to me, he weakly kicks out at my head before stepping to the center of the trampoline.

"Bigham," Connor says, looking down at me, "if you come up on this trampoline and fight me, you're just going to get knocked out. If you don't come up here, I'm going to jump off of this thing and just beat the shit out of you until they call the cops, then I'm going to bury you."

I am still holding Travis's flask like an idiot.

"Bigham, do not go up there," says Travis, who has walked up to stand beside me. Usually he'd only be up this close to the trampoline to get the best view, but I think he's really worried about me. "He won't even let you get up there before he punches you, then he is going to kill you," Travis says.

"This is yours," I say, as I hand him the flask. "Travis, I'm tougher than I once was. I bet I'm even stronger than him in some respects," I say, tired of standing there like a confused puppy being coaxed between two prospective owners trying to prove who cares for me the most.

"Bigham, no. It doesn't matter how strong you are now. You've never thrown a punch, and you've never been punched. You are thinking in hit points, and fights don't work that way. Dude, look at his hands," says Travis.

Connor's hands are huge. The police will be able to iden-tify his knuckles when they pour plaster into the indentations he's about to make in my face. I hop up onto the trampo-line and, for some reason, take off my white work shirt and undershirt, tossing them back over my shoulder to Travis like a bouquet. It's so bright up here on the trampoline, and the faces of everyone who's gathered around the trampo-line are so dark, and since the lights are behind my antag-onist I can't distinguish any features in his face, and it feels like I'm just fighting Connor's shadow as he leaps across the trampoline to tackle me.

Connor expects to knock me down with this tackle, and he grunts from the impact and maybe surprise when I stand my ground, and there is a long second, a delicious indeci-sion of physics where we strain to see who will have momen-tum as his mistress and she takes a thoughtful pause then chooses me. I lift Connor from his crouch and push him up until he's standing. He's still trying to push me over, but to save him the embarrassment of trying to tackle me again, I turn my hips and let him fall off of the trampoline.

People are still coming out of the house as news of a fight travels through the upper floors. I see Tad Simpson cheer from behind his girlfriend as she leans topless from the window of Kyle's parents' bedroom, and they might be fucking while we fight. Once Connor hits the ground I hear some people cheer and clap, but I don't think it's for me. I think it's because they know this fight now has to escalate beyond a shoving match.

"Holy crap, it does look like the octagon," says some guy behind me.

Connor full-on leaps back onto the trampoline and grabs me around the waist and picks me up and slams me down with what they call in Greco-Roman wrestling "grand amplitude"—an amplitude so grand that it almost drowns out the sound of my spine hitting the aluminum ring of the trampoline. It stuns me and I inhale harder than when I prepared for my birth wail, though I somehow manage to kick out from Connor's grasp and start to crawl across the trampoline so I can try to vomit over the side and spare us the indignity of having to avoid a puddle of celery and peanut butter puke draining through the center of the ring during our entire fight. As I'm crawling away, Connor grabs me by my ankle to drag me back toward him.

"Oh no, Big Ham," he says. "Never." I zoom back across the trampoline because the weight of Connor kneeling in the center makes it a downhill slide, plus my sweat has slickened the entire trampoline like it's the frying pan in Paul Bunyan's mess hall. I am pulled back so fast my mind is fooled into thinking that Connor has superhuman strength, and I growl and backhand Connor so hard that he sits back in the middle of the trampoline, his hand clutching his face, and then the Bigham is upon him.

I straddle Connor and cuff the baseball hat from the top of his head, and it rolls across the trampoline to Travis, who still holds my shirt in his hands. Now he has an article of clothing from both fighters, and if he's lucky I'll autograph mine after the bout. I lean back and ball my right hand into a fist, and I finally get to full-on punch Connor in his face.

"And they thought I was going to shoot you," I say.

It is then that I become the captain on the bridge of the battleship *My Fist*, hovering in low orbit above the planet Connor. And I punch Connor twice, once in his eye socket, so hard that I could have used the extra second to bore into his brain if I wasn't pulling back for my second punch, which glances off his cheek. Connor grunts and his arms flail about, but it turns out that his flails hold as much force as my most concentrated punches, and though the first wild blows succeed only in threshing the sweat from my chest hair, he soon regains his senses and scoots back from between my legs and starts punching me in the stomach.

In the seventh grade, my class went to the state museum on a field trip, and they had an exhibit that showed the British bombardment of Fort Moultrie during the Revolutionary War. There was either a model or a painting of a British ship with its cannons blazing on the wall in front of us, made to look like it was off in the distance, and to the front of the exhibit there was an actual wall of palmetto logs representing the side of the fort that faced the sea. The reason why there's a palmetto tree on our state flag is because the spongy and resilient nature of the palmetto logs actually caused the cannon balls to either stick into or bounce off of the walls of the fort, whereas a more brittle wood would have splintered and collapsed underneath the British assault. At this moment I like to think of my midsection as a wall of palmetto logs because even though Connor just got like twelve solid punches in a row on me, I am merely disoriented and out of breath, but if I were thin every single rib would have been broken.

Also on this same museum field trip the tour guide told us that the attack was led by Admiral Peter Parker and I said, "Hey, like Spiderman," and I was shushed by Ms. Meadows, even though I was the only one paying enough attention to the tour guide to say something even remotely related to what she was talking about. I use the additional adrenaline inspired by the memory of this injustice to collect my wits and punch Connor back, but the trampoline under him absorbs most of the impact, and if we had thought to build Fort Moultrie's walls from trampolines maybe we could have sent those cannon balls right back at those ships and wouldn't have had the fort taken in the ensuing siege of Charleston.

Just the fact that I remember that exhibit is part of the reason why I'm fighting Connor right now, because if I had spent more time on field trips like those trying to make friends or talking to girls then I wouldn't be here at seventeen fighting Connor on a trampoline just because I missed a kiss from the first girl who could bear to get close to me.

I crab walk off of Connor and around his head, miraculously getting him, for a second, in a sleeper hold. While he struggles I fiercely whisper into his ear, "Go to sleep, Connor. Dreamland is missing its princess," but in reality I barely manage a hoarse "fuck you." Connor laughs and easily peels my forearm from under his chin.

Connor bucks under me and with both hands at once pushes me back and then gets on top of me, and at this point I learn the difference between the strength of a guy who's just started lifting weights six months ago and the strength of a guy who has a much bigger frame and has been naturally athletic for his entire life. He tries to put me in a choke hold, but I am thrashing my head around and cursing him, almost getting a mouthful of his armpit hair, which smells like spruce needles and molten salt.

Connor gives up trying to rip my head off and raises his fist, the houselights glinting from the thick hair around his wrists. These testosterone gauntlets simply scream survival of the fittest. His chin is bigger, his tendons are thicker, his chest is broader, his girlfriend is the hotness, and he even has better one-liners than I do, and now all these factors are pouring through his arm like hot lead and pooling and cooling in his knuckles. Connor smiles as he starts to punch me into extinction. My stomach crumples under him because I am the guy who knows what our state motto means and he is the guy who hung a heavy bag up in his garage. *Dum Spiro Spero* means "While I breathe, I hope." And I can't breathe, so I don't hope.

During this beating I somehow manage to look past Connor and see the bright white crescent moon in the deep blue springtime sky, shining its hardest on our backyard brawl so the stars can see clear enough to place their bets. The reason why there's also a crescent moon on our state flag is because it's the last thing a dumb moonshine-soaked South Carolina farm boy remembered seeing after he challenged a fit British professional soldier to fisticuffs on the night before the actual battle. It's the most intense pain I've ever felt in my life, and Connor will not stop. The give of the trampoline is the only thing keeping me from getting knocked out. I groan and roll over onto my belly, still between his legs, and Connor keeps hitting the back of my head and then starts hooking his punches to get at the side of my face.

"Ahhh, Connor, stop," I say, in a deep, dazed voice like he's just trying really hard to wake me up and I want that last five minutes of sleep. "Stop, Connor, man. You win. I give up," I say.

"Ugh!" Connor says, punching me hard in my back. "Ugh, ugh, ugh, ugh, ugh!" he says, punches punctuating each ugh. "One, two, three, four, five, smart guy! Did you think I could count that high?" he asks, punching me again in the back after asking me that question.

"Yes, I know you can count that high. You're not dumb. I'm dumb. I'm dumb because I tried to fight you," I say, telling him what I guess now was exactly what he wanted to hear because he stops punching me.

"I bet you can't count that high because you were too busy getting knocked out!" And he pauses and puts his hands on my back to help himself stand up, and the entire party cheers. I hear Connor jump down onto the wet grass, and then I hear people giving him high fives. Through the trampoline's netting I can see the light-up boomerang thing that hit Joanna, and it is still blinking. I roll off of the trampoline and stumble toward Kyle's house but both of my eyes are swelling shut. Somebody throws an empty beer can and it hits me in the back.

"Bigham, it's Travis," says Travis, grabbing me by the arm as I walk up the deck steps.

"Travis, can you get my keys out of the key bucket so I can go home?" I ask, wiping a grab bag of face fluids—blood, sweat, drool, snot—from my chin and flicking them from the back of my hand where it lands hissing into the grill.

"Bigham, you got rocked!" shouts Cody Fulmer from inside the house through the open sliding glass door. He is our school's fullback, and his nickname is just "Fullback" in place of his last name.

"Thanks, Cody Fullback," I say, giving him the peace sign.

"Dude, you can't drive. You can barely even see," says Travis. Everybody has left the deck, and I think it's because people are embarrassed to be around me.

"Can you give me my shirt?" I ask.

"Connor took it from me," says Travis and I turn around, and the last thing I can see before almost going totally blind from eyes swelling shut is that Connor has tied the sleeves of my shirt around his neck to make a cape and is shotgunning a beer in the center of the trampoline.

"Bigham, I should call your sister or someone to come pick you up," says Travis.

"My sister's in Florida with her boyfriend. Please don't call my parents. I just need a place to sit down," I say.

"Jacob, do you need to go to the hospital? Do you think you might have a concussion?" asks Naomi.

"No, I'm just totally beat up," I say, and I can sense that her fingers are about to touch my face so she can try to look into my eyes, but I jerk my head away, and even though this is just a reflex to avoid pain, I will count it later as a spurning of Naomi's insistent physical advances.

"Travis, take him upstairs to my room." It is Kyle's voice.

Travis grabs me by my wrist and takes me through the sliding glass door, back through a mass of people that I can hear gasp as they get a good look at my face under the indoor lights.

"Kyle, dude. I'm really sorry," I can't help but say as I follow Travis up the steps.

"Jacob, can you even see?" asks Travis as he opens the door to Kyle's bedroom. "Connor really went to work on you."

"Yeah, I can see, just not well enough to drive home," I say, sitting down on Kyle's bed. "Can you get me some ice so I can get the swelling down and then get beyond out of here?"

"OK, I'll be back," says Travis, closing the door and leaving me in the light of Kyle's aquarium.

When Travis comes back he's got paper towels wrapped around two lumps of ice. I thank Travis, and when I put the ice up to my eyes, I can smell baby powder and Naomi's perfume.

"Did Naomi wrap these ice packs?" I ask Travis.

"Yeah," says Travis. "Hey, I'm going down to get your keys, then I can drive you home."

"Naw, man, just let me rest here for a little bit. I can barely move," I say and I lie back on Kyle's bed.

"OK, just don't go to sleep, man. If you have a concussion, you'll go into a coma and you might die," says Travis. "Let me know when you're ready to get out of here," Travis says, and after he closes the door I lie back and hope for a coma.

CHAPTER 11

When I wake up the next morning I am not at all disoriented. I know that right here, sitting on the edge of Kyle's bed—huffing chunks of blood-crusted snot into tissues that I toss into Kyle's tin Batman trashcan— is the closest I'll ever get to fucking Naomi. Kyle has his own bathroom, and I dump the tissues into the toilet before peeing for what seems like days. There was also an empty soda can in the trash, and I rinse it off in the sink and then fill it with cold water because I am such a big thirsty baby.

The cold water surprises my stomach, and I end up retching most of the water back into the sink before filling the can again and sipping. While drinking in front of the mirror, I feel my first twinge of disorientation because my face is just a total wreck. Not only have I woken up in another person's room, but I also look like another person. I discover that the combination of dehydration and my still-spasming stomach has brought out my abs to an unprecedented degree. It looks like I just had a bunch of elective surgery done, and while the liposuction healed overnight, the half-gallon of collagen I had injected into my lips, cheeks, and brows will still take weeks to heal.

Across the hall I can hear a man and a woman talking to each other. Every few seconds one of them giggles. These giggles belong to Kyle and Naomi. They are in the computer room across the hall, he in the leather chair and she in his lap, both wearing bathrobes. On the left side of the desk is a plate holding a half-eaten stack of homemade blueberry pancakes. On the right side of the desk Naomi's bra is hanging from the corner of Kyle's graduation cap. Naomi is scrolling through a folder holding hundreds of photos taken last night. Kyle is pulling back the top of Naomi's bathrobe to kiss her shoulder. They are so completely into each other, teasing each other, being happy together. They must have been like this all morning. If flirting were carbon monoxide, I would be dead right now.

I feel guilty for spying on them for what must have been less than three seconds, and I turn to rush down the steps, but Kyle hears my footsteps and calls from the computer room.

"Bigham, is that you?" he asks.

"Yeah, Kyle, it's me," I say, shouting from the stairwell. "Listen, I'm going to just head on out. I'm sorry for making a complete jackass out of myself."

Kyle comes out of the computer room. "We're just glad you're alive. We checked on you a couple of times during the night to see if you were still breathing." He tosses me an undershirt that must be his Dad's. "Hey, check out the pictures from last night," he says, beckoning me toward the computer room.

I put on the shirt and follow Kyle, because even though I don't want to speak to anybody who saw me at this party *ever* again, Kyle's been so nice to me that I can't be rude and leave. Naomi is sitting on the loveseat next to the computer chair with her robe wrapped tighter around her. The black lace doily choker thing is pulled lower down her neck, neatly bisecting a deep red hickey. An elastic strap peeking out from behind her back shows that she is sitting on her bra. This is the first time I've seen her without makeup. She gasps when she sees me.

"Oh my gosh, he really hit you," she says.

"Yes," I say.

"Bigham, look at this," says Kyle at his computer. He scrolls down to a picture of Connor and I squaring off across the trampoline. The picture is titled "The Main Event," and it must have been taken from inside the gazebo. You can only see my back and a small halo of light shining on top of my shaved head, and the shadows are so sharp that you can barely see Connor's face, just his shoulders and shins. The most surprising thing about the picture is that it doesn't look like I have no business trying to fight Connor. It looks like we're two evenly matched fighters, he with the reach advantage and I with a little more muscle.

"Kyle, I am really embarrassed about fighting at your awesome party," I say.

"It's OK, Bigham," says Kyle. "Look at this awesome picture. I'm going to e-mail it to you."

"And Naomi," I say, turning toward her, "I spent all year trying not to look like some psycho in front of you. I was not even going to talk to you at this party. I was just going to come and chill out and prove that I could get along with people, and now I look exactly like the kind of person that you should be afraid of," I say.

She and Kyle have graduated, and this will probably be the last time I ever get a chance to talk to them, and I want to use this time to prove that I realize just how much of a fuck-up I am.

"I mean, you were my first real crush, and Connor was my first real bully, and I couldn't handle either one. All I've done my whole life is read and play video games in my room in a log cabin, and you guys seem light years ahead of me as people even though I'm about to be a senior. You gave me this shirt," I say to Kyle, pulling out the front hem of the shirt to show Kyle which one I'm talking about. "You gave me that ice," I say to Naomi.

"Jacob, it's OK," says Naomi. She gets up from the loveseat with one hand still clasping shut the top of her bathrobe, and she puts her other hand on my shoulder and squeezes.

"You shouldn't have to be like my parents," I say. "I haven't helped or been a friend to anybody this year. Everybody's just had to deal with me."

"Bigham, it's all right," says Kyle, looking up from his computer chair at Naomi then at me. "A lot of people did a lot of embarrassing things at that party."

"I'm going to leave, OK?" I say. "Thanks for letting me sleep."

"OK, Bigham," says Kyle. "Listen, I'm sorry, but some-body puked in the key bucket this morning, and yours was one of the only sets left. I put them in a bowl with some dish-washing liquid right by the sink."

Downstairs there are still some people passed out on the couches. I dry off my keys on a paper towel and then load Kyle's dishwasher for him. I also grab a trash bag and fill it with any beer or soda cans I see.

Travis calls my house about two weeks later. There have been about five calls since ten o'clock in the morning, cut-ting off just as the answering machine comes on.

"Hello, is this the House of Bigham?" asks Travis when I finally pick up.

"Travis? Have you been calling all morning?" I ask.

"Yeah!" says Travis. "Why didn't you pick up? Were you still asleep?"

"No, creditors have been calling the last few days, and if you want to talk to us you have to leave a message so we can call you back," I say. "Mom missed a payment on the computer or something, and now we get calls all the time."

"Does your face still look like Connor smashed his fist into it like fifteen times before he got out of breath and you pleaded with him to stop punching you?" asks Travis.

"Yes, Travis. Maybe because that is what literally happened to it. You didn't substitute in a new expression about my beat-to-shit face. You just asked me if it looks how it looks," I say. "If a car ran over your arm I wouldn't ask, 'Dude does your arm still look like a car ran over it?' I would ask if your arm looked like a possum…" and I trail off, caught.

"That got ran over by a car?" asks Travis, putting me in my place, because that's the only thing that happens to possums.

"OK, well, I would have thought of a different simile," I say.

"Does your face still look like a ham piñata?" asks Travis.

"It looks bad. It's much better now, but like when I got home I couldn't lie to my Dad, and Mom almost cried when she saw me the next day. I just outright told them that I got in a fight at Kyle's party. I didn't tell them who it was with; I just said that the other guy was a bully who had pushed me around and then hit a girl I was with." Which is kind of true.

"Are you grounded or something? I dropped by your work, but your manager said that you quit," says Travis.

"No, I think my Dad was just grateful that I took my aggression out in a way that didn't make the newspapers," I say. "Plus, they could tell that I was really embarrassed."

"They could tell that you were pretty beat up about it?" Travis asks.

"Nice," I say.

"Well, at least you're alive. I came back to wake you, but Kyle said to let you sleep. You know Joanna, that girl Connor hit with the Frisbee? We waited for like four hours, but you were out for the duration," he says.

"Oh man, I never called her," I said. I had really wanted to, but I figured that she had probably seen the fight and figured that I was some lunatic. I didn't want to call because then she might think that I was stalking her and it would be like Naomi all over again.

"Bigham, that's part of the reason why I called you. She doesn't think you're crazy, and you're welcome to still call her. But Joanna and I hadn't seen each other for so long. It was like four in the morning and we were out by the gazebo," says Travis, trying to soften the brag.

"Let me guess. You made out with her," I say, totally prepared for Travis to behave like Travis.

"Yeah. That and she totally blew me," says Travis. "She told me not to tell anyone, especially not you, but I figured you should know."

Thank you, Travis. Thank you for turning what would have been my first kiss into your third blowjob.

"That's fine. Whatever. I mean, it really doesn't matter what I think," I say.

If only I could keep firing after first shooting myself so that I don't just slump over after the first bullet but somehow manage to empty the entire clip, not just using the gun to kill myself but to totally physically excavate my head of every memory.

"Bigham, if it's any consolation, she wasn't really that good," says Travis.

"Travis, please don't complain about getting a blow job." To me, somebody complaining about how a girl gives you a blowjob is like someone disparaging the cut and clarity of the diamonds in their Super Bowl ring.

"It's not all bad news, man," says Travis. "Everybody was talking about how cock diesel you looked fighting Connor. Super ripped. Are you on steroids or something?"

"No, but thanks for the compliment," I say. "Did you see Connor when you went to the grocery store?"

"Yeah. He's got a shiner too. He also showed me his back where you pushed him into the trampoline. There's a huge purple welt from one hip to the other," Travis says.

"I would go down and apologize to him, only I don't want to be seen back at the grocery store," I say.

"Hey, are you near a computer? You should get online and check out the pictures on Kyle's site," says Travis. "There's this one awesome one of Connor that might make you puke."

On "The Party" page at Kyle's website there's a side panel that you can scroll down to see all the pictures from the party, but the first picture you see centered in the main area of the page is a picture of Connor right after our fight. He is sitting in the beerbarrow, his lower back resting on the pile of ice. He still has the sleeves of my shirt tied around his neck and is holding a can of beer in his right hand and smiling, his left arm around Angela, who is bent over beside him, pressing another can of cold beer against his black eye. She is pursing her lips in total concern, oblivious to the breasts about to pop out of her top. The heat from Connor's back is causing steam to rise from the ice and up into the night air, and now I know that by trying to fight Connor I had only set in motion the events that would lead to him being the centerpiece in the coolest picture ever taken of some-one from Stonewall. There he is, shrouded in the skin of his victim, pounding down his victor's liquor under the tender administrations of his otherworldly girlfriend, ensconced in a throne of his own steam.

"Oh, dude, there was another picture after that one that Connor's girlfriend made Kyle take down. She was leaning over Connor when her tit popped right into his open mouth, and he turns to the camera with it still in his mouth and gives the thumbs up. After that people practically formed lines to high five him that entire night. The picture's awesome. I'll e-mail it to you," Travis says.

"No thanks, Travis," I say. "You've done enough. You have called and told me everything I never wanted to hear in about five minutes." I really want to yell at him, but he may be the only person I'll see this summer besides my parents and I want to keep that option alive.

"Hey, what I really called about was to see if you wanted a job," says Travis.

"Blah blah blah," I say. "I got a job for you. Joanna already gave me your job, job on my knob, I get it," I say.

"No, seriously, Bigham. My mom works for the Parks Department. They're about to start a summer camp, and they are really hurting for counselors. We could work together for the entire summer, and it's like the easiest job in the world," says Travis.

"Travis, I don't know anything about kids," I say. "Don't we have to be trained to work with them? Don't we have to know CPR or first aid or something?"

"No, we really don't do that much at all. Like, I'm going to be in charge of them in the computer lab, and you can play kickball with them. There's a camp organizer and some counselors already there. We would just follow their lead," Travis says. "You make minimum wage, though. Like you make no money." Even though Dad hadn't been yelling at me for not having a job, I still felt like I needed to get out of the house, and a stack of my résumés was on the kitchen table, and I had just taken a test at Red Lobster yesterday, even though I didn't trust myself to an entire summer of resisting their biscuits.

"These kids aren't like troubled or anything?" I ask.

"No, they're normal. But it's in town, so I feel the need to warn you that ninety-five percent of these kids will be black," Travis says. "And by that I mean one hundred percent of these kids will be black. I mean, the place that we're applying to, one of its initials stands for 'Empowerment' so you know it's totally black."

"I'm sure race will be the least of the many reasons causing me to hate and fear those kids," I say. "Is the job a guaranteed thing and I just have to show up?" I ask.

"No, my mom's not running the program. We still have to fill out forms and get an interview and everything," Travis says.

The next day I pick Travis up from his house and we drive into town. I had told Travis to dress up for the interview even though he thinks that he has this job on lock. Travis does not have a résumé of his own and has to use the same teachers that I use as references, even though one teaches honors history to me but couldn't pick Travis out of a police lineup, which is a good thing considering Travis had hung a baseball bat out of the passenger side window of Tad Simpson's Ford Explorer and annihilated that teacher's mailbox the summer before. The woman who interviews us has her office adjacent to Travis's mom. Travis waves says hi to his mom and takes a piece of candy out of the jar on her desk, which he sucks on during our entire interview, and on the way back to the interviewer's office, one of his dress shoes slips off because they are his father's.

"This interview is not a formality," says the woman, who is black and in a tan business suit. She has the job application forms we filled out in the waiting room. I am nervous about my form, because even though I was not fired from either job, I listed the reason for leaving from the grocery store as "I had irreconcilable differences with a fellow coworker." I hope that just the fact that I spelled "irreconcilable" correctly will help her overlook how I couldn't keep my shit together in the high-pressure field of bagging groceries and mopping. Now that I think about it, the phrase "fellow coworker" is pretty redundant, and if she's the kind of person who's impressed by a correctly spelled "irreconcilable," then she also knows I'm just inflating my language to try to impress her. This interview is a chess match that she's won before I even make my first move. I am so tempted to pick up the trash can and tell Travis to spit his candy into it.

"But I'm not going to grill you either," says the woman and smiles. "I just want you to know that even though you're Patricia's son, we care deeply about who looks after our children at the center," she says, nodding toward Travis. "You'll be in charge helping to make sure that about a hundred kids are kept safe and have fun for the entire summer," she says.

"Travis," she says, addressing him, "you'll be in charge of projects in the computer lab. And Jacob," she says, turning toward me after looking down at my application, "you'll take care of all the outdoor activities, like kickball and field day and so on. You both can work together to help organize arts and crafts," she says. "Now, do you think you can handle that? A lot of people come in here and think that this is a do-nothing job, but you're going to be in charge of our most precious resources here," she says, interlacing her fingers and waiting for one of us to respond.

"Sure," says Travis, and I wonder if he can hear me rolling my eyes.

"Travis and I would be very excited if we were given the chance to work here," I say, leaning forward in my chair. I figure that the best way to make a positive impression is to preemptively refute all the negative things she is already thinking about us. "We are not here just to goof around and let these kids run wild. We both know what it's like to go to summer camps where you can tell the counselors don't care and are just there for a paycheck, and we've resolved to really pay attention to what these kids need."

"That's good to hear," says the woman, pushing aside our applications and looking at me.

"I know that this will, in fact, be harder than any other job I've had before," I say. "A mistake here is way different than squashing a loaf of bread or letting a thirteen-year-old into an R-rated movie. These are these kids' most formative years," I say.

Travis turns to me right then, even though the woman is about to ask another question, and says, "You are totally rocking this interview, Bigham."

"And Travis, what about you?" she asks. "Do you feel you can contribute to this camp, to make it a safe and fun learning experience?"

"Totally," says Travis. "The computer lab will not be a problem. I believe that I can successfully instruct these children in computers for the entire summer," says Travis.

"Fine," she says. "Miss Grier is the one in charge of the entire camp, and you can both meet her down at the center on Monday at 8:00 a.m. before the children start signing up," she says.

"Thank you, ma'am. We'll do our best," I say, and Travis tries to high five me, but I am already standing up to shake our interviewer's hand.

On Monday Miss Grier asks us which group we want to be in charge of. There are a little over one hundred kids sitting on three metal bleachers inside the gym, divided by age group. Miss Grier is shorter than Travis and I, dressed in shorts and a T-shirt from a 10K run for leukemia. She is thin and obviously fit, black with tightly bound short cornrows, tough-eyed enough to let us know with a glance that we fall below her initial expectations for camp counselors, but nice enough to greet us warmly and give us each a neon yellow plastic whistle on a black nylon lanyard.

"I gave you guys the blue group," she says. "They're the eight to twelves, and though there are more of them, they might be the easiest to get a handle on," she says, pointing to the kids on the middle bleacher. They are entirely preoccupied with each other, they probably know one another from previous years at this camp, and the only one looking at us is a kid who is brushing green sugar from the bottom step of the bleacher with his sneaker onto the gym floor below. The sugar had spilled out from a Pixy Stix and there is only the sound of shouts and the scraping of sugar grains over the aluminum steps in the gym.

"Darrell!" shouts Miss Grier at the kid, who looks up guiltily and begins to bend down and use his hand to brush away the sugar. Miss Grier spies the pack of Pixy Stix peeking out from the top of a girl's purple backpack. "Mr. Jacob, can you go get those Pixy Stix for me?" she asks. I had just left a job where I was a bagboy, and the disconnect between going from a job with "boy" in its title to being referred to with a "mister" causes me to pause for a second. I used to listen for the crinkle of chip bags and the hissing of popped soda tabs as a cue to ask people at the theater to throw away their outside food or drink, but that only made me the most unpopular usher for a single showing. What Miss Grier is asking me to do will make me the most unpopular counselor for the entire camp.

I walk up to the girl sitting next to the purple backpack. "Sorry, but I gotta take these things," I say, motioning toward the bag of Pixy Stix.

She takes a second to snap the last bright pink barrette into her friend's hair then turns to pout at me as I reach for the bag.

"You'll get them back at the end of camp today," I say, but I don't know the official camp policy on contraband candy. The Pixy Stix might be gone for good. Her friend starts to laugh at her until Amaya punches her in the shoulder, then Amaya turns to stare at me with a squinched-up face of little girl hate.

"Don't pout, Amaya," says Miss Grier.

Travis is holding his hand out for a Pixy Stix before I give the entire bag to Miss Grier.

Miss Grier has the entire camp line up from one end of the gym to the other so that the counselors and the campers can introduce themselves. Travis and I walk down the line shaking hands and asking their names in what I guess to be just an entire camp exercise in politeness. Amaya refuses to shake my hand.

"C'mon, Amaya, shake Mr. Jacob's hand," says Mr. Travis.

"Not until I get my candy back," Amaya says, crossing her arms.

"If I give you your candy back by the end of the day will you shake my hand?" I ask, and Amaya nods.

I make two of the little kids from green group laugh when they stick out their hands to shake at the same time, and I grab both them in my right hand and shake up and down really fast. The thirteen- to fifteen-year-olds are in the back of the line. The guys are to the very back. I know Travis will comment to me later about one of the girls in line who has massive breasts at age fourteen, but during the entire process he is remarkably civil, and the kids start to like him because they know that with Travis they will be able to get away with anything. Some of the fifteen-year-old guys are taller than both of us, and one crunches Travis's hands in his grip and Travis cries out in what is definitely not mock pain. I had already shaken that kid's hand, and maybe he had taken it easy on me, or maybe I was stronger than he was. Either way, we now know why Miss Grier is in charge of red group.

Darrell is also at the very end of the line, joking around with guys from red group. "Darrell, aren't you supposed to be in the line with the rest of blue group so that we know you're with us?" I ask.

"Dude, I'm thirteen in August, so I might as well be back here," says Darrell, calling me out in front of all the oldest guys, and I wonder if he knows that the same sickness that gave us both pubic hair is also compelling me to try to impress the oldest guys to Darrell's detriment.

"Don't call me 'dude.' Get back in line with blue group," I say, crossing my arms in front of my chest. Darrell stares at me for a second while the older guys start laughing behind him before he storms out of line and down to blue group, and I distinctly hear him mumble the word "white" under his breath when he walks past me, and I want to sit him down and let him know that what compels me to behave like this is not the legacy of hundreds of years of racial oppression, but rather millions of years of the dynamics of male dominance. However, I am standing here in my nicest pressed pair of khakis and a brown and white polo shirt, with a shaved blonde head and my arms across my chest, while Darrell is a thin black male in an Orlando Magic basketball jersey, so I do look like a stereotypical South Carolina state trooper who has just waved away the brother of somebody who has just assaulted a cop and was running up to explain everything. I feel bad for Darrell and look back to blue group to see him standing behind Amaya. They are brother and sister.

"So how does it feel to be the most hated man in the Harris family?" asks Travis when we are outside after lunch. It is supposed to be an hour of free play, but the kids left a bunch of trash under the picnic tables and in the fenced in dugout beside the baseball field, so I have asked them to help me pick up "every scrap of it" (Jesus) before play because "we need to respect this place during our time here" (Christ).

"The who family?" I ask, holding open the trash bag as a boy, Raj, dumps in a small carton of orange juice. I thank him.

"Darrell and Amaya. They think it's going to be a tough summer with you acting like this," Travis says.

"Well, how do you expect me to act, Travis? Do you want them to just throw trash all over the place and eat Pixy Stix while Miss Grier's talking to them? I mean, you heard Miss

Grier about how we're supposed to keep things in order and help instill community values and stuff like that. So that's what I'm doing. And if we don't do that the first day, then everything with them is going to be harder as time goes on," I say.

"Yeah, but we're young guys. We can be like the cool counselors," says Travis.

"How cool, Travis?" I ask. "How cool do you need to be? Did you bring your flask? You can pass that around. That would be so awesome," I say.

"Listen, Bigham. I know that you think I'm lazy and you think that I'm not going to contribute to this job. You think I'm going to drag you down and make us look stupid," says Travis. He's right. I don't think he has any discipline or initiative, and when I see him I see myself a year ago, only he smoked and took caffeine pills in front of his computer while I stuffed candy bar wrappers into a Pringles can next to my PlayStation.

"Travis, I do need you to be the cool guy here," I say. "I'll help you keep this job, but it's obvious from my years at Stonewall and my hour and a half here that I will not be liked."

"I already told Darrell that you were just trying to keep everything in order," says Travis. "Or something. I also said you were kind of a jerk but that you would mellow out," he says. "Honestly, I have no idea what I'm doing here. There's over thirty of these kids, and I'm in no way an authority figure."

"OK. That's fine, I mean I don't want to spend the summer yelling at them, but that's a big part of our job," I say.

I hear something land on the roof of the baseball dugout. Somebody had accidentally thrown a foam three-pronged glow-in-the-dark boomerang-like device up there. It is one of the newest toys and highly prized. One of the kids, James, is already scaling one of the gutters to get to it.

"Hold on, James," I say. "That's dangerous. Let us get it." Travis and I walk over to the dugout. I make a step out of my hands to boost Travis on top of the roof, and from there he tosses down the boomerang AND a Frisbee that apparently went missing last year, which is still so full of pollen that when I catch it a cloud of yellow powder launches into my nostrils and Darrell falls to the ground laughing.

That afternoon the entire camp walks down the block to learn about the community garden. After a volunteer from the Parks Department talks to us about bees being the angels of agriculture each kid gets to pick a single vegetable from the garden and put it in the basket that Travis is holding. Everything is going fine—no plants are getting trampled, and Miss Grier is giving us the thumbs up—when we hear Amaya scream by the compost heap. I drop a squash and run over to where she is hopping on one foot.

"What's wrong, Amaya?" I ask, looking for blood or if her limbs are hanging at odd angles.

"I was trying to squish a spider and I lost my shoe," says Amaya. She is on the verge of tears. She points toward the compost heap, where there is a small depression where her shoe was sucked down and the compost has closed over it. I reach my hand in and yank out her shoe, shaking coffee grounds from the glittering face of a Disney princess.

"Here you go, Amaya," I say, handing her the shoe.

"I'm not wearing that! It stinks now!" she says.

"It only stinks because your feet have been in it," I say, trying to joke with her. The entire camp laughs, except for Amaya, who is now way beyond the verge of tears.

"Amaya, I am sorry I said that," I say. When I give her back the Pixy Stix at the end of the day she still refuses to shake my hand.

So on the first day I made Amaya cry, and as the weeks go on some additional events conspire to make me ludicrously, intensely, ridiculously unpopular with blue group. A counseling group run out of the local YMCA comes one morning to talk to the camp about respecting yourself and playing well with others and then finally preventing sexually transmitted diseases, which I think is a bit much for the eight-year-olds, but we still separate the boys from the girls and let each half of blue group get talked to. The girls handle it fine, but I've already had to tell the boys to quiet down twice, and when they hand out the AIDS prevention pamphlets, some of the guys promptly roll them up and start hitting each other with them as Travis and I watch from across the gym.

"Look at them, Bigham. They're hitting each other with the anti-sex pamphlets," says Travis. "Next they'll be fucking each other with the anti-violence pamphlets."

"Guys, give me those," I say. The woman giving the lecture has already had to tell them to settle down while I was walking across the gym and is obviously flustered and wiping her glasses off with the tail of her T-shirt and mumbling to herself.

"Ma'am, I am ashamed of the way these guys are acting," I say, loud enough for all of them to hear. "I don't think they deserve whatever you were going to give them after this," I say. She had already given the girls T-shirts and Airheads, and these are huge post-lecture rewards, and I may have just endangered my life by taking them away from the guys. I have to ask Travis to go outside and make sure that the girls have already eaten their Airheads so as not to remind the guys what I've denied them.

That was the first of two post-lecture prizes that I had to take away in the first month. When the firefighters had a puppet show, they had asked blue group questions about how to avoid burning to death and threw foil packs of trading cards to the kids who got them right. Since Raj was the only one paying attention, he got like five packs of what turned out to be wrestling cards, which he didn't like, so he handed them out to the kids around him, and for a second it was fun to watch the scaffolding of an entire wrestling card economy get thrown up around Raj, even while the foil wrappers still fluttered beneath the bleachers.

The kids are shuffling through the cards while Miss Grier thanks the firemen who are packing away their wheeled-in puppet stage. Then Steven's eyes go wide as he finds a card that shows a match between two girls, and all I hear is the word "thong" before Miss Grier walks up and motions for Steven to give her the card. She takes the card and shows it to me and asks, "Can you believe that?" and I agree. That card is scandalous. So I have to go around and get any of the wrestling cards that have girls on them, which is an immense boost to the kids' not entirely untrue perception of me as a tightly wrapped buzzkilling shithead.

Then, while the firefighters are leaving, the guys start acting like the favorite wrestlers they've traded for. Steven is now mock elbow dropping Raj, going "wa-bow, wa-bow," and almost pushes him to the gym floor.

"These kids are going nuts," says Travis, looking up from the girls on the wrestling trading cards.

"All right," I sigh. And now I have to go through blue group getting every wrestling trading card.

"Hey, man, why are you taking all our cards away?" asks one of the firemen. "I thought the lady in charge only wanted the cards with women on them taken away."

Goddamn it, fireman. Quit giving me a hard time while I'm trying to keep these kids from suplexing each other into the water fountain.

"Well, these cards show almost unattainable physiques and inappropriate behavior for both men and women," I say. "They're obviously starting a riot around here, and so I think it's best that they all be taken up." Michael is holding his last card, a reflective one of Diamond Dallas Page, in his hands. He is holding those hands palms outward, with the pointer fingers and the thumbs touching so that the space between them is in the shape of a diamond. Diamond Dallas Page holds his hands like that and then head butts through his hands, thereby shattering into shards a symbolic diamond all over the arena with just the strength of his skull. In the center of Michael's diamond glitters the last wrestling card in the room, and I know that if I try to take this last card from Michael he will try to head butt my hand.

"Michael, please hand that card to me," I ask, but Michael just smiles from beneath his outstretched hands. "Michael, if you try to head butt my hand when I take that card, all you're getting is knuckle. It is going to hurt," I warn him.

"Why are you always taking stuff from us, man?" asks Darrell. Michael still refuses to give me the card. He is in the center of the top rung of the bleachers and is very hard to get to.

"Don't make Mr. Jacob spear you!" says Travis, and the guys in blue group all start shouting, "Goldberg! Goldberg! Goldberg!" and it is the first time in my life where I have been referred to as a wrestler whose primary gimmick wasn't being overweight. Well, Dad used to call me Hulk Hogan if he wanted me to help him carry wood in, which is the same strategy I employ in order to get Michael down from the top of the bleachers.

"C'mon DDP! C'mon down here Diamond Dallas Page!" I say, waving Michael toward me. Michael gets up and holds his card above his head like the championship belt, displaying it to his left and his right. He jumps off the side of the bleachers and rushes toward me.

Michael is eight years old and the smallest guy in blue group, so all I do is hold my hand against his head and watch him swing wildly for my body. Everybody laughs, but then I let Michael grab my arm and twist as hard as he can, and I go down to one knee, feigning pain, feeling how much stronger I am in comparison to him, and I realize that this is the first physical contest I've ever been in where I didn't fear losing or getting hurt, but only worried about my opponent having fun and saving face. He is wailing away on my arm with one of his skinny elbows and I barely feel it. With a flick of my wrist, I twist out of his grasp, but the back of my hand barely grazes his face and I knock out one of his baby teeth.

"Oh my God," says the oldest girl from blue group, Chanterelle, holding her hand over her mouth as if to protect herself from another one of my jackhammer blows. She is the most mature kid in blue group and the one Travis and I keep asking when we forget another camper's name. She is almost like a third counselor, and to see her this shocked at my behavior is more embarrassing than I thought possible. I charitably give her an excuse to scamper from out from the shadow of my unforgiving fist.

"Chanterelle, can you please go get us some paper towels, please?" I ask before turning to Michael. "Mike, are you all right? I'm really sorry, Mike. That wasn't one of your permanent teeth was it?"

Michael shakes his head and I am relieved to see that he is not crying. He is already examining his knocked-out tooth and is holding the wrestling card over his mouth, dotting it with blood and causing it to no longer be a point of contention in blue group.

"You see, guys, this is what happens even if you play fight," I say, taking a damp paper towel from Chanterelle and wiping the blood from Michael's face. He shies away from the towel, embarrassed, and I pat him on the shoulder and give him another paper towel to wrap his tooth in before asking him to sit down.

"Bigham, you might be the worst camp counselor ever," says Travis.

Each day one of the three groups gets an hour in the computer lab with Travis, where he asks them to find a picture of somebody that they admire on the internet, paste it in Word, and then type under it why they admire that person. However, he forgot to turn on Google's Safe Search when they first started and was instantly greeted with a Photoshopped picture of Beyoncé doing something a woman of her caliber would never consider.

I am in charge of kickball, and I spend most of the time instituting rules that an experienced counselor who had refereed kids before would have laid out on the first day, like no sliding. Michael came hauling ass to home one day, and I could tell he was about to slide headfirst, and with a speed and strength I never knew I possessed, I dashed out to grab him under his armpits and lift him up, his legs still pumping as I spun him around, dissipating his momentum.

"Dang, Mr. Jacob, c'mon!" he screams, but I know that if he had slid I would have spent the next half hour breaking up an impromptu Easter egg hunt for his deciduous teeth.

"And no, not even feet first!" I say, envisioning black calves sheared down to the universally red meat beneath the skin, clouds of pink home plate dust settling into scrapes that spell my name.

"Also, nobody throw the ball at the head or else the out doesn't count," I say, after Darrell chucked a ball so hard at Tamara that I could not tell which object depressed more from the force—the rubber or her skull. Tamara is like 5'9 and is a star athlete. She shakes it off, but still I have to walk over to Darrell.

"Darrell, you can't throw the ball as hard as possible. You, you personally, Darrell, have to go easy on these other kids," I tell him.

"If they don't want to get hit, tell them to play another game," he says.

"Darrell, let me see that bicep," I say. Darrell is always flexing his bicep, which, though smaller than mine, is more impressive because his isn't covered by a scruff of flab-stretched skin that looks like the shaved wattle of an albino basset hound. Darrell pushes back the sleeves of his screen-printed Dragon Ball Z button-up shirt and his bicep jumps up. I reach out to squeeze it.

"See?" I say. "That's super Saiyan. You know that you are the strongest and the oldest out here, and so I'm going to depend on you to hold back that strength." I see it as my singular duty at this camp not to create another Connor.

"Just because I'm bigger doesn't mean I'm going to pretend to lose," says Darrell.

"At kickball? Darrell in two months you're going to be out of this group. In a year you're going to be stronger than I am. You're like, redshirting it here in blue group. So please, do not kill Raj with that ball, or throw hard at girls, OK?" I ask.

"OK," says Darrell, nodding.

Coming up with ideas for arts and crafts is hands down the most difficult part of the job for Travis and I because we were both the kinds of kids who never neatly cut down the lines or pressed hard enough with the crayons. We spend a week just using paper plates. First, we make a submarine porthole out of a paper plate by cutting out the outside rim, painting the rest of the plate blue, then decorating that plate with construction paper fish. We then put the plate in plastic wrap and staple the rim to let these kids get a rare glimpse of the strange and wondrous creatures of the deep. It is pretty lame, and what's best is when the kids call me out on it and Travis agrees.

"I don't even know what a porthole is, Bigham," says Travis in front of everybody in blue group. This is worse than the time that he said the ham sandwiches in the lunch packs they give to the kids were terrible and that he was going to Arby's and if anybody else wanted something to just give him the money and he'd bring it back. Any counselor who brings restaurant food into a lunch pack scenario obviously has no respect for the spirit of day camp. The kids wouldn't stop asking him for curly fries, and I finally had to ask Travis to eat his meal outside.

On Monday of the following week, Travis and I start passing out paper plates again and everybody groans. But then we bring out the mixing bowls and spoons and chocolate chip cookie mix and everybody cheers! Travis and I then take turns loudly deciding between us who should have each job in the cookie-making process, making sure to mention a positive quality about each camper we assign the job to.

"Hmmm…" Travis says, "we need some of our best readers to take turns reading out these directions."

"You're right, Mr. Travis," I say. "I wonder… who would do a really good job at this?" And, of course, Raj and Chanterelle raise their hands because they are natural leaders. We give the egg-breaking jobs to our quietest campers, including Janette who regularly checks up on her younger sisters in green group and who I suspect comes from an abusive family because one time when her dad picked her up I saw him lift her by the left shoulder strap of her pink overalls and toss her into the backseat while yelling at her sisters. Also, he threw an almost empty Gatorade bottle into the bed of my truck when he thought nobody was looking, and I can tell how attached I am growing to these kids because my anger at both events is now almost equal.

Michael is a mixer, Kiyana is a dolloper (one who dollops), and we are almost out of roles when we get to Darrell.

"While these cookies bake, you know, there's going to be people from red group and green group who are going to try and get at them," I tell Travis.

"We need like, a cookie guard," says Travis. "Like a tough dude." And Darrell raises his hand. That afternoon I bring a cookie home to Mom and tell her how her advice probably saved my entire summer. It is the first time I see her cry since she thought I might be an irredeemably savage sociopath who was going to kill the entire class of 2001.

On the next-to-last week of camp, Dad takes me to Outback Steakhouse. It's just me and him because Mom is visiting Julie who, in the spirit of our family's tradition of her doing everything a million times better than me, has just flown in from her summer mission trip to Wales.

"You're not ordering a salad or anything like that, OK Jacob," says Dad as we drive into town. "I know you're try-ing to stay slim and everything, but the word 'steak' is in the actual name of the place." Dad is excited because he believes that Sumter can actually call itself a town now that it has an Outback Steakhouse.

"Nope, I'm going to order a big old steak," I say. "I am going to eat every bite."

"Look out at those fields," he says, pointing to my right. "Before I was stationed down here they were all woods. And do you remember when they used to be cotton? Now they're all ginkgo. You know the FDA never said that ginkgo cured anything? They don't know if it works at all."

"Yup," I say, looking out at the rows and rows of ginkgo plants, the setting sun glinting from the chest-high sprinklers that line the edge of the field, like automated lasers programmed to keep the tiny trees in line.

"Next year all that will be houses," he says. "With streets like Hickory Street and Cotton Street."

"Gingko Lane," I add. This is all coming from a man who doesn't believe in global warming. I wonder how many topics Dad thought to talk to me about while he was out on his route today.

At Outback the food arrives and Dad takes off the brace he's had to wear since he hurt his wrist delivering phonebooks so he can get a better angle at his steak. Before I eat I notice that I am almost as thin as he is and if he died tomorrow I'd be able to fit into his second suit, which is a good thing because I've lost enough weight to be swimming in mine. And then I am ashamed of myself for thinking of him dying when the steak that he hurt himself working for steams in front of me. And then I feel additionally awful because I'm comparing what might be the start of my prime to what may be the beginning of his decline and I'm still nowhere close to as tough as he is.

"Go ahead, Jacob, eat up," he says, stopping to shake some salt into his beer. "I'd buy you one of these, but I still have to wait a couple years," he says.

"I am. I'm just going to wait a little bit until it cools," I say.

"I didn't mean to bring up your weight on the ride over here," says Dad. "I was just trying to say something about how much weight you lost."

"I know, Dad. I know it was kind of a compliment," I say, picking up my knife and fork just to appease him.

"You know, for a while there Mom and I were worried that you were exercising so much and not hanging out with your friends. I mean, I was proud that you were working and getting in shape, but I thought it might have had something to do with how I yelled at you after that disaster with that girl," says Dad. "I wanted to ask you about it, but I also didn't want you to stop doing all those positive things for yourself. That's part of why I wanted to get out tonight—to talk to you about it." I put my knife and fork down again because I know that getting a substantial paragraph from Dad that doesn't involve Earl Scruggs or growing tomatoes is kind of a big deal.

"Dad, don't worry about it," I say. "I was a lazy jerk and I didn't even know her that well, and I deserved to be yelled at for how I treated my teachers. This girl, she was just the first one that I actually really liked. I just didn't expect to like her that much, and when she wouldn't be my girlfriend, I didn't know that I would react that badly," I say, my voice cracking like a forty-five-year-old man's wrist under the weight of every name in the tri-county area.

"Jacob, I know. And I should have thought about it like that at the time," says Dad. "You know what girls are like?" he asks.

"No," I say, tearing my eyes away from my steak. Even though it's an emotional moment, I'm still hungry, and I hope that Pavlovian principles don't dictate that I start salivating when Dad begins to give advice.

"Girls at your age are like model airplanes," says Dad.

"Ugh," I say to myself.

"Imagine that you and every guy around you were suddenly obsessed with model airplanes," says Dad. "You couldn't stop thinking about them, you couldn't stop talking about them. You looked them up on the computer and you stared at them all the time at school, and the first time a friend of yours made one he was a hero." I'm just glad he hasn't made jokes about wanting to make a model airplane and a corresponding need for something like his wrist brace.

"Heck, there are some times where you think about model airplanes so much that you need one of these," he says, picking up his wrist brace. I kind of laugh.

"So what would be the first thing you're going to try to do?" he asks.

"I'm going to go and try to make a model airplane," I say.

"Right," Dad says. "And the first time you try, everything's just going to fall apart," he says. "And your second one's going to look like shit," Dad says, laughing into the top of his beer before taking a sip.

"But pretty soon they'll stop being model airplanes and start being women who understand you," Dad says. "Well, your mom does. None of the other ones really gave a damn, but you know."

"Thanks, Dad," I say. "But maybe you should have yelled at me earlier. I mean, in only a year I've worked two jobs and I'm in the best shape I've ever been in," I say. Sometimes I do think about why Dad didn't yell at me more while I was growing up. Why didn't he yell about how much of a fat, conceited slug I was becoming?

"You know, Jacob," Dad says, "I was tempted to maybe give you a harder time before about, um, your physical condition and what I thought was you being lazy. But you did so well at school, which I never did, and you weren't a mean guy and you didn't get in trouble a lot. Your mom reminded me that I built that cabin out there in the woods so nobody could bother us or tell us how to live, so I figured I'd let the weight and all the video games go as long as you weren't a bad kid, which you weren't. But when your guidance counselor called, I got kind of scared that I had actually let it all go too far."

"I wasn't going to hurt anybody. I was just a crybaby," I say.

"You are an emotional dude," says Dad.

CHAPTER 12

My most emotionally trying time as a camp counselor came on Thursday, right before the day we're supposed to go to see the double Dutch competition. It is free play time right after lunch, and I am swinging the kids around in the parachute. The parachute is a about the size of a table cloth, stitched from triangles of red, yellow, and blue nylon. Kids are supposed to grip the handles on the sides of the parachute and use it to bounce a beanbag up into the air, but I have no idea about how the rest of the game is supposed to go. Instead I've devised a game called "Angry Rainbow" where one kid sits in the center of the parachute and I bundle all of its handles in my fists, wrapping the kid in the parachute. Then I swing the kid around in circles like twelve times before slowly bringing the parachute to a stop. It is a popular game and makes me feel strong. It is a game that a dad would think up.

"Grrrr...I am an angry rainbow, and I will spin you to your doom!" I say to Michael, who is in the parachute for a second turn. I've spun around ten kids and I'm getting tired.

"OK, guys, I'm pretty wiped out. No more Angry Rainbow for today," I say. I set Michael down and he stumbles out, dizzy. I am about to go get a drink from the water fountain near the doorway to the gymnasium when I feel somebody grab my arm. It is Amaya.

"Mr. Jacob, you can't stop playing Angry Rainbow. It was about my turn to go," she says, still holding my arm. I turn around and kneel in front of Amaya, like a server at a table in a family-style restaurant as part of my ongoing effort to adopt a posture of genuine interest, instead of standing there with my arms folded like the King of Siam. Plus, I'm glad that Amaya and I are starting to get along and that she uses my name for the game and didn't ask just to be swung around in the parachute.

"Amaya, you have already been on it, and I am too tired," I say. "But I'll remember for tomorrow and you'll be the first one I swing, OK?" I say.

"Aww!" Amaya says and pretends to pout. She is still swinging my arm back and forth, as if trying to prime it for another round of Angry Rainbow. "Just remember that you promised," she says before skipping off. She actually skips off. This from the girl who called another girl whose mom was white a "yellow belly" before pouring nail polish into the girl's purse. In Amaya's defense that girl was being a jerk to her that day.

When I walk over to the water fountain, Mrs. Robbins, who is the counselor in charge of green group, is standing there staring at me, her whistle lanyard wrapped twice around her right hand. Mrs. Robbins is very strict with her kids. She's worked at this camp for years, and there's one fifteen-year-old in red group who could probably lift a picnic table over his head but regards Mrs. Robbins with a respect bordering on terror.

"Jacob, I have some concerns about what I just saw over there," she says in a tone that transfers some of the gray in her hair to mine.

"Mrs. Robbins, I know that game looks unsafe, but the grass is high, and I checked it for glass or anything," I say. "I'm careful not to swing too fast."

"No, it's not the game, even though it does look dangerous," she says. "I'm talking about the way you and that child were touching," she says. "I think it's inappropriate, and I don't want to see any more of that. In fact, if I do see it again I'm going to tell Pamela about it and you and she can talk," she says. I am caught completely off guard by this.

"Um, Mrs. Robbins, Angry Rainbow is not, like, a slang term," I say. "It's really just a game."

"I'm not talking about that game, Jacob. That kind of affection from a male camp counselor just doesn't look right," she says. "This and the fact that these campers still talk about you knocking out Michael's tooth make me wonder about you," she says.

"She was just holding my arm," I say. "And that incident with Michael was a total accident."

"I'm just warning you that I care about these children enough to confront people when I think something inappropriate is going on," she says, and she turns to walk back into the building.

I lean against the water fountain and tell myself, "Just don't explode, just don't explode." I was taking part in something that should have looked idyllic, that should have proven that I was a hardworking and considerate counselor, and now I'm being accused of both hitting and molesting children. This isn't like high school where I either wanted to punch or fuck everybody I saw in the hallway.

"Mrs. Robbins, before you go," I start to say.

"You can protest all you want to, but I saw what I saw," she says. "I draw the line because I know where it should be."

"Before you go I want you to know that what you saw was only what you saw. There's been no other touching and there won't be other touching, and not because of what you or what anybody else says but because I wouldn't do something like that. I don't care what you report because I know that I haven't done anything wrong"—which is exactly what a child molester would say.

The next day ours and a dozen other camps run by the county are going to watch the double Dutch competition at the convention center. We have lined up our camp outside the exhibition center, and while Miss Grier and Mrs. Robbins go inside to check in and see where we are assigned to sit, Travis and I have to go down the line checking to see if anybody has gum, water pistols, do-rags, or anything that might could be construed as gang insignia. I have to ask Darrell to put his do-rag in his pocket.

I actually want to watch the competition because after learning to jump rope myself I can now find value in seeing a sport I've struggled to get better at taken to its limits, instead of my once instant dismissal of sports as just athletic people doing what they were good at. But during the competition, all the kids can think about is spending the money their parents gave them at the concession stand, so every ten minutes I have to form like a wagon train of ten kids to navigate through the crowd of other campers so they can get cotton candy to throw at each other. I ask Chanterelle to help keep track of which of the blue groupers are in the restroom because Travis is too busy flirting with one of the counselors from the camps in the next section. Some guys our age all the way from Korea are competing, and they have their hair styled in outrageous ways, and some of the girls from blue group are trying to hold Travis's up like that just with their hands. This elicits a pigtailed giggle from the blond camp counselor from Roaring River, and now Travis will be useless to me at least until lunch. The kids from the Roaring River group each have bright yellow camp T-shirts that have a group picture of the entire camp printed on the front, and each camper got to personalize theirs with glitter and puff paint, which makes me feel extraordinarily self-conscious about how raggedy our camp sometimes looks. Roaring River also has a hugely muscular camp counselor barking out orders, his shoulders cracking apart the barely dried puff paint tiger pacing down his spine. However, when one of the Korean kids tries to do a front flip over his partner but fails, landing on his lower back and getting whipped by a few whirls of the ropes before his partners can stop them, his kids laugh while my kids gasp.

Lunch is going to be the most trying time for us because every camp has to go outside and eat their food under awnings while the Parks Department cooks hotdogs and hamburgers. There are a bunch of field day activities set up outside that every camp can go visit—an egg toss, a Frisbee throw for distance, a blow-up castle. Mrs. Smith, the director of the entire camp program, takes some counselors from each individual camp aside and assigns them to different activity stations. Travis and I are asked to bring out coolers and folding tables, and I am hefting down a cooler full of juiceboxes from the back of a school bus when Mrs. Robbins walks up to me.

"Hey, Jacob, I really need your help," she says. "Those kids over there by the air castle simply will not listen to me. Almost all of them are from other camps and they are running wild. I'm afraid they'll hurt one another," she says. "I turned around for one second and this big kid got into the castle and got everybody riled up."

"Well, I'm sure if you report it to Miss Grier she'll be able to bail you out," I say, and I can hear Travis's end of the cooler hitting the ground as he lets his handle go, surprised at my back sassing. I haven't told Travis about yesterday. When I drove him home, I waited until he got out of my truck before bursting into tears.

"Jacob, Miss Grier is inside talking to the director of the entire program, and if they come out and see what's going on, we're all going to be in trouble," she says. "Listen," she says, pulling me aside, "I'm sorry about what I accused you of yesterday. I probably went too far when I said it and I'm sorry. But I'm too old to be yelling and yanking kids off this blow-up castle while they jump around, so will you please help me?"

"Are you sure you trust me over there by that castle with all those kids? Because a blow-up castle is remarkably similar to an air mattress you...suspicious bitch!" I say in my head before actually saying, "OK."

"You got this cooler, Travis?" I ask.

"Sure, as long as you don't catch another beat down on that trampoline," says Travis.

The air castle looks like an actual castle being invaded at a one-sixth scale, packed with kids pushing one another inside and out, its side netting straining with screeching faces and scrabbling hands. Mrs. Robbins and I stand there for a second, our hands on our hips, disapproving of the entire crusade.

"All right!" I shout with my deepest voice. "Everybody needs to get out of that castle."

"Shut up!" shouts what must be the castle's king, a fourteen-year-old from Roaring River, his yellow shirt completely devoid of puff paint, except for a red circle with black horns drawn around his own face in the group picture.

I look him square in the eye and point right to him. "*I am* telling *you* to get out of that castle, and if you have a problem with what I say, you can come out of there and say it straight to my face," I say, in a firm but even voice. He stops jumping up and down and stares at me like he's going to leap out at me, but instead he storms out of the castle.

After the rouser leaves ,the rabble begin to untangle themselves and pile out. Some are pretty scuffed up, and when Michael tumbles down the yellow and red steps I look to see if he's still in one piece.

"Mike, are you all right?" I ask, and he nods yes. "Was there anyone else from blue group in there?" I ask, and he shakes his head no.

"Somebody's hurt in there, though. Do you hear him crying?" Michael asks.

In the center of the castle is a heap of bright yellow, topped with a bowlcut lump of sandy blond hair. He looks about twelve but is even bigger than I was at his age. He might be even heavier than I am now, and when he leans back to cry harder, his neck, which is facing me, folds its fat into a second sobbing mouth. He has his hands down around his ankle, which I hope isn't broken.

I take my shoes off and walk to the steps of the castle. Without the weight of the other kids, the castle is beginning to collapse. It must have had a sprung a leak a long time ago, but as the kids kept coming in the their weight must have let the remaining air keep the castle upright.

"Kid, are you OK?" I ask, standing in the entranceway. I laugh to myself and try to sound dramatic, like a firefighter in the movies. "Kid, you gotta get out of here! This whole place is about to come down!"

"I'm going to suffocate if this thing falls on me!" the kid says. "But I can't move because I think I might have torn my Achilles tendon," and right then I know he doesn't have a broken ankle if he can still get out words like that. I am holding up the doorway as he says this, the anti-Samson, propping up both gut-punched pillars as the castle tries to sag into the grass. The anti-Connor.

"C'mon, kid, you're gonna be fine. Just crawl toward me," I say. He turns to slowly drag himself across the trampoline, and I would make fun of him in my head to pass the time, but my brain is too busy empathizing with him utterly. When he finally gets to sit on the castle steps, I pat him on the shoulder.

"All right, here, I'll help you get back to Roaring River," I say. I help him up and he puts his arm around my shoulder, and as I help him limp back to the Roaring River awning, I feel a paperback novel in the pocket of his cargo shorts flopping against my leg.

"Thanks," says the kid, and that was it, that was his last breath, and now he is completely out of breath as he sits in his counselor's lawn chair, his legs splayed. The counselor thanks me too before bending down to examine the kid's ankle, and I can tell by his exasperated interrogation of the kid that the counselor has been fed up with what this kid's fat antics for weeks.

"I think I tore my Achilles tendon," says the kid, chewing on the straw of a juice box that he had just suckled until it collapsed like a one-six-hundredth scale of the castle.

"Thanks for the diagnosis," says the counselor, rolling his eyes at me, a gesture that includes me in a fit society where citizens like him feel the need to try to wash the blubber from the gutters of his muscular metropolis.

"You'll be fine, kid," I say, and then I jog over to where the rental equipment guys are smoking by their truck to ask them if they can blow up the castle again.

I am looking at my watch and counting down the three minutes that this group of ten kids gets in the reinflated castle when Travis walks up behind me. I've decided that after three minutes most of the fun jumping stops, and the kids either get exhausted or start to push each other down.

"Bigham, the kids all have their food now. They're all quiet and there's plenty left over for us, so I figured we'd walk over and get some," he says.

"Thanks, Travis," I say. "This group is almost done."

"OK," says Travis. "I also came to see if there was any end to your vengeance."

"What are you talking about?" I ask.

"That kid in the blow-up castle! Connor punches your lights out on a trampoline so you break his brother's ankle on one?" Travis asks.

"That kid was Connor's brother? I thought he looked familiar," I say. Only I didn't think he looked familiar because he looked so much like Connor, but because he looked so much like me.

On the next-to-last day of camp Travis calls my house at seven thirty in the morning.

"Travis, please don't tell me you're calling in sick on the last day of work," I say.

"No, Bigham, I'm calling to tell you not to pick me up this morning. My parents got me a car yesterday, so now it's finally my turn to drive," he says. "Can you meet me at the road because my car is kind of low and I don't want to smash it on the roots in your driveway?"

"Which road? Do you mean the paved road or the dirt road that you turn on to get to my driveway?" I ask.

"Oh shit, I forgot you guys live in the 1940s. I can't have all that red dust on my new car, Bigham," he says. "Sorry."

"Dude, I'll just drive then," I say.

"No, never mind. I'll meet you at the end of your driveway," Travis says.

Travis's new car is like a '94 canary yellow Chevy Corvette that his dad must have bought from another guy on the air force base. It's still got a "My other car is an F-16" bumper sticker, and those air force guys are always selling their cars.

"This ride..." I say, "is pretty boss." Travis nods.

"Thanks, Bigham," he says. "Hey, I really wanted to drive you because I got the car for holding down a job, and you're the only reason I got to work in the morning," he says. "I'll buy you lunch at Sonic or something too," he says, which is epically considerate for Travis.

"Thanks, Travis," I say. "Well, you got me the job in the first place."

"The whole summer was pretty easy, though," Travis says. "Except for coming up with crafts, and you did most of that," he admits.

"Yeah," I say, "When you talk to girls, you're probably going to turn this summer into a story about how you worked with underprivileged kids."

"They weren't underprivileged," Travis says. "They had the privilege of working with us."

I am kind of nervous this morning because as a treat for the kids we're taking them to the bargain matinee at the theater I used to work at. When I get out of the bus to buy the tickets, Miranda is still working in the ticket window, and I can see her Tupperware tub of popcorn in the seat next to her.

"Hey, Miranda, how's it going?" I ask.

"Just fine, sir. Got the whole family out here, don't we?" says Miranda, not recognizing me in the slightest. There's a pretty high turnover rate at the theater, and once we get inside I don't see Lawrence, or Nate, or anybody who might know me. I am no longer an usher, and today I don't have to act like one either because the kids are well-behaved, especially those in blue group, and I actually wish someone here recognized me. I eat popcorn and watch Pokémon while Travis goes to Bojangles.

That afternoon is our last craft and we make flowers for Miss Grier, with green pipe cleaner stems and delicate crepe paper petals, and Darrell is so fascinated by the crepe that he makes a huge, heavy, flawless white orchid that the girls in blue group coo over to an embarrassing extent. I make two flowers: one a bright orange for Miss Grier that I put with the others in a glitter-painted cardboard vase, the other a pale periwinkle that I still keep pressed between the pages of the owner's manual in the glove compartment of my truck. It's to give to someone—a girl who I've actually talked to and who likes me afterward—and when I remember that's it there for her, I'll open the glove compartment and paw through parking tickets and expired insurance cards until I find it.

Made in the USA
Charleston, SC
12 February 2014